WHY FRIENDSHIP MATTERS

More anthologies available from
Macmillan Collector's Library

Food for Thought

The Joy of Walking

The Art of Solitude

WHY FRIENDSHIP MATTERS

MATTERS

Selected Writings

Edited and introduced by
MICHÈLE MENDELSSOHN

MACMILLAN COLLECTOR'S LIBRARY

This collection first published 2020 by Macmillan Collector's Library
an imprint of Pan Macmillan
The Smithson, 6 Briset Street, London ECIM 5NR
Associated companies throughout the world
www.panmacmillan.com

ISBN 978-1-5290-3265-9

1 3 5 7 9 8 6 4 2

A CIP catalogue record for this book is available from the British Library.

Casing design and endpaper pattern by Andrew Davidson
Typeset in Plantin by Jouve (UK), Milton Keynes
Printed and bound in China by Imago

Contents

Introduction
MICHÈLE MENDELSSOHN

The history of humanity is the history of friendship. In the twenty-first century, friendship's affectionate bonds may seem devalued by the cynical operations of digital networkers – the strangers who send you Facebook messages that read, 'Hi, my name is Anna, friend me!' But it's precisely because of the sluttish availability of weak digital relations that true friendship matters more than ever. It has an existential magnitude that a mouse-click will never touch.

Nevertheless, online 'friends', those ghosts of the real thing, can feel like sad reminders of our loneliness in the modern world. Yet this feeling is not, in fact, new at all. 'A Crowd is not Company, and Faces are but a Gallery of Pictures ... where there is no *Love*,' Francis Bacon observed in the seventeenth century. Digital technology is only the latest method for reminding us of this timeless fact of life.

The amazing growth of online 'friendships' does, of course, sometimes lead to real-world friendships. Before I relocated from Edinburgh to Salt Lake City for work, I went online, met a Greek-American doctor called Nikki who ran a social club, and a few days after my plane landed we were sharing sticky homemade baklava. Ten years and several relocations later, Nikki remains one of my sweetest friends, part of a cherished circle of international relations loosely held together by WhatsApp groups, long phone conversations and the occasional face-to-face visit. I'm reminded of our digital chats when I read the letters that make up Jane Austen's *Love and Freindship*.

Some of the earliest discussions of friendship occur in the works of classical writers – Plato, Aristotle and Cicero. The Renaissance essayist Montaigne, who features in this collection, reinterpreted their ideas to speak to its highest form: the friend as soulmate. Why did he love his friend? Montaigne asks himself. 'Because it was he, because it was I.' There was no simpler, but no more authentic, answer. This is what Aristotle would call true friendship because it is grounded in compassion and mutual sympathy. Centuries later, across the Atlantic Ocean, Anne of Green Gables yearned for just that when she wished for 'a bosom friend—an intimate friend, you know—a really kindred spirit to whom I can confide my inmost soul.' And in mid-twentieth-century New York City, a young Audre Lorde counted herself lucky to find such a friend. She describes the encounter as nothing short of life-changing. It should not surprise us that ancient philosophers, iconic heroines, and civil rights activists aspire to the same ideal. The desire for friendship is universal.

Still, friendship conforms to no universal system or law. There are friendships of utility: such as the royal companions and confidantes of the high and mighty, which Francis Bacon and Alice Emma Ives describe. 'I hate the prostitution of the name of friendship to signify modish and worldly alliances,' the American philosopher Ralph Waldo Emerson writes. Those who share our cares may also help us better ourselves, he explains in his essay. His compatriot, the runaway slave Harriet Jacobs, shares a moving account of the gentle woman whose kindness and conversation restored her to herself. For too long, it was thought that women couldn't be friends with each other. With a few exceptions, this nonsense seems to have prevailed until the nineteenth century, when women writers began to push against that notion, as journalist Alice Emma Ives does in the essay included in this anthology. The splendour of women's friendships is revealed in Audre Lorde's contribution.

Friends may be a comfort, but they can also provide a valuable source of discomfort. The writers collected here admit to the invigorating effect of a friend who is willing to hold up an honest mirror to our flaws. We needn't agree with them, of course. We may, in fact, prefer to go on believing a pretty lie rather than an ugly truth. James Boswell's eighteenth-century diary captures a lively debate between Samuel Johnson and Oliver Goldsmith on friendly disagreements.

There are, however, limits to what we should endure from, or for, our friends. Someone who uses their intimate knowledge of you against you is nothing more than a frenemy, Oscar Wilde warns in his fairy tale 'The Devoted Friend'. Avoid self-interested fakes who slither up to you and say, 'a true friend always says unpleasant things, and does not mind giving pain.' Watch out for those injuries and offences that can turn friendship into hateship.

Most of all, guard against slow-killing neglect. As Samuel Johnson wisely notes, 'the most fatal disease of friendship is gradual decay.' You know the drill: your friend has a baby or gets a new job and then progressively fades out of your life and into a world of playdates or blue-sky-thinking boardrooms. Something will need to be done to avert the inevitable decline and fall. But *what*? The novelist Sarah Orne Jewett suggests meeting somewhere different, going outdoors, breaking bread together. Good fellowship is the food of friendship.

'The mere names of our friends might for many of us almost tell the history of our own lives,' Anne Thackeray Ritchie writes. 'As one thinks over the roll, each name seems a fresh sense and explanation to the past.' Make a list of all the friends you have ever had – from day one to today – and you'll find you've written a mini-autobiography. Our existence is the sum of our relations. Friends are the family you choose.

'The charm of friends in pen and ink is their unchangeableness,' Ritchie observes, and that makes them some of the best friends one can have. The writings included in this volume will, I hope, also be a friend to you. Let these chapters be a tonic when you need one, a comfort when you want it, and a place to put your cares away. In each chapter, you'll discover a new companion, or visit with an old familiar. You may want to read them all at once or dip in and out. Though you may neglect them, they will always be there for you: ready to advise, to talk to you directly and intimately, to make you ponder, wonder or break out in laughter.

WHY FRIENDSHIP MATTERS

Jane Austen
1775–1817

Despite their genteel presentation and satirical style, Austen's works are timeless meditations on social relations, psychology and institutions. She began writing in her early teens and produced *Love and Freindship*, reprinted here, when she was fourteen. *Sense and Sensibility*, *Pride and Prejudice*, *Mansfield Park* and *Emma* were completed when Austen was in her thirties. They demonstrate her rare ability to portray the everyday in uncommonly interesting ways. A shrewd observer of humanity's foibles, Austen often cast a satirical eye on Regency society, hilariously anatomizing the age's sentimental excesses and domestic pieties. In *Love and Freindship*, a melodramatic and often misspelt correspondence records friends' adventures, precisely timed visits and fainting spells with mocking astringency. The result is a brisk send-up of the conventions of amiability and romance that G. K. Chesterton called, 'a thing to laugh over again and again.'

LETTER the FIRST
From ISABEL to LAURA

How often, in answer to my repeated intreaties that you would give my Daughter a regular detail of the Misfortunes and Adventures of your Life, have you said "No, my freind never will I comply with your request till I may be no longer in Danger of again experiencing such dreadful ones."

Surely that time is now at hand. You are this day 55. If a woman may ever be said to be in safety from the determined Perseverance of disagreable Lovers and the cruel Persecutions of obstinate Fathers, surely it must be at such a time of Life.

Isabel.

LETTER 2nd
LAURA to ISABEL

Altho' I cannot agree with you in supposing that I shall never again be exposed to Misfortunes as unmerited as those I have already experienced, yet to avoid the imputation of Obstinacy or ill-nature, I will gratify the curiosity of your daughter; and may the fortitude with which I have suffered the many afflictions of my past Life, prove to her a useful lesson for the support of those which may befall her in her own.

Laura.

LETTER 3rd
LAURA to MARIANNE

As the Daughter of my most intimate freind I think you entitled to that knowledge of my unhappy story, which your Mother has so often solicited me to give you.

My Father was a native of Ireland and an inhabitant of Wales; my Mother was the natural Daughter of a Scotch Peer by an Italian Opera-girl—I was born in Spain and received my Education at a Convent in France.

When I had reached my eighteenth Year I was recalled by my Parents to my paternal roof in Wales. Our mansion was situated in one of the most romantic parts of the Vale of Uske. Tho' my Charms are now considerably softened and somewhat impaired by the Misfortunes I have undergone, I was once beautiful. But lovely as I was the Graces of my Person were the least of my Perfections. Of every accomplishment accustomary to my sex, I was Mistress. When in the Convent, my progress had always exceeded my instructions, my Acquirements had been wonderfull for my age, and I had shortly surpassed my Masters.

In my Mind, every Virtue that could adorn it was centered; it was the Rendez-vous of every good Quality and of every noble sentiment.

A sensibility too tremblingly alive to every affliction of my Freinds, my Acquaintance and particularly to every affliction of my own, was my only fault, if a fault it could be called. Alas! how altered now! Tho' indeed my own Misfortunes do not make less impression on me than they ever did, yet now I never feel for those of an other. My accomplishments too, begin to fade—I can neither sing so well nor Dance so gracefully as I once did—and I have entirely forgot the *Minuet Dela Cour*.

Adeiu

Laura.

LETTER 4th
LAURA to MARIANNE

Our neighbourhood was small, for it consisted only of your Mother. She may probably have already told you that being left by her Parents in indigent Circumstances she had retired into Wales on eoconomical motives. There it was our freindship first commenced. Isabel was then one and twenty. Tho' pleasing both in her Person and Manners (between ourselves) she never possessed the hundredth part of my Beauty or Accomplishments. Isabel had seen the World. She had passed 2 Years at one of the first Boarding-schools in London; had spent a fort- night in Bath and had supped one night in Southampton.

"Beware my Laura (she would often say), Beware of the insipid Vanities and idle Dissipations of the Metropolis of England; Beware of the unmeaning Luxuries of Bath and of the stinking fish of Southampton."

"Alas! (exclaimed I) how am I to avoid those evils I shall never be exposed to? What probability is there of my ever tasting the Dissipations of London, the Luxuries of Bath, or the stinking Fish of Southampton? I who am doomed to waste my Days of Youth and Beauty in an humble Cottage in the Vale of Uske."

Ah! little did I then think I was ordained so soon to quit that humble Cottage for the Deceitfull Pleasures of the World.

Adeiu

Laura.

LETTER 5th

LAURA to MARIANNE

One Evening in December as my Father, my Mother
and myself, were arranged in social converse round
our Fireside, we were on a sudden, greatly astonished, by hearing a violent knocking on the outward
door of our rustic Cot.

My Father started—"What noise is that," (said
he.) "It sounds like a loud rapping at the door"—
(replied my Mother.) "It does indeed." (cried I.) "I
am of your opinion; (said my Father) it certainly
does appear to proceed from some uncommon violence exerted against our unoffending door." "Yes
(exclaimed I) I cannot help thinking it must be
somebody who knocks for admittance."

"That is another point (replied he); We must not
pretend to determine on what motive the person
may knock—tho' that someone *does* rap at the door,
I am partly convinced."

Here, a 2^d tremendous rap interrupted my Father
in his speech, and somewhat alarmed my Mother
and me.

"Had we not better go and see who it is? (said she.)
The servants are out." "I think we had." (replied I.)
"Certainly, (added my Father) by all means." "Shall we
go now?" (said my Mother.) "The sooner the better."
(answered he.) "Oh! let no time be lost" (cried I.)

A third more violent Rap than ever again assaulted our ears. "I am certain there is somebody knocking at the Door." (said my Mother.) "I think there must," (replied my Father.) "I fancy the servants are returned; (said I) I think I hear Mary going to the Door." "I'm glad of it (cried my Father) for I long to know who it is."

I was right in my conjecture; for Mary instantly entering the Room, informed us that a young Gentleman and his Servant were at the door, who had lossed their way, were very cold and begged leave to warm themselves by our fire.

"Won't you admit them?" (said I.) "You have no objection, my Dear?" (said my Father.) "None in the World." (replied my Mother.)

Mary, without waiting for any further commands immediately left the room and quickly returned introducing the most beauteous and amiable Youth I had ever beheld. The servant, she kept to herself.

My natural sensibility had already been greatly affected by the sufferings of the unfortunate stranger and no sooner did I first behold him, than I felt that on him the happiness or Misery of my future Life must depend.

Adeiu

Laura.

LETTER 6th
LAURA to MARIANNE

The noble Youth informed us that his name was Lindsay—for particular reasons however I shall conceal it under that of Talbot. He told us that he was the son of an English Baronet, that his Mother had been many years no more and that he had a Sister of the middle size. "My Father (he continued) is a mean and mercenary wretch—it is only to such particular freinds as this Dear Party that I would thus betray his failings. Your Virtues my amiable Polydore (addressing himself to my father), yours Dear Claudia and yours my Charming Laura call on me to repose in you, my confidence." We bowed. "My Father, seduced by the false glare of Fortune and the Deluding Pomp of Title, insisted on my giving my hand to Lady Dorothea. No never exclaimed I. Lady Dorothea is lovely and Engaging; I prefer no woman to her; but know Sir, that I scorn to marry her in compliance with your Wishes. No! Never shall it be said that I obliged my Father."

We all admired the noble Manliness of his reply. He continued.

"Sir Edward was surprised; he had perhaps little expected to meet with so spirited an opposition to his will. "Where, Edward in the name of wonder (said he) did you pick up this unmeaning gibberish?

8

You have been studying Novels I suspect." I scorned to answer: it would have been beneath my dignity. I mounted my Horse and followed by my faithful William set forwards for my Aunts.

"My Father's house is situated in Bedfordshire, my Aunt's in Middlesex, and tho' I flatter myself with being a tolerable proficient in Geography, I know not how it happened, but I found myself entering this beautifull Vale which I find is in South Wales, when I had expected to have reached my Aunts.

"After having wandered some time on the Banks of the Uske without knowing which way to go, I began to lament my cruel Destiny in the bitterest and most pathetic Manner. It was now perfectly dark, not a single star was there to direct my steps, and I know not what might have befallen me had I not at length discerned thro' the solemn Gloom that surrounded me a distant light, which as I approached it, I discovered to be the chearfull Blaze of your fire. Impelled by the combination of Misfortunes under which I laboured, namely Fear, Cold and Hunger I hesitated not to ask admittance which at length I have gained; and now my Adorable Laura (continued he taking my Hand) when may I hope to receive that reward of all the painfull sufferings I have undergone during the course of my attachment to you, to which I have ever aspired. Oh! when will you reward me with Yourself?"

"This instant, Dear and Amiable Edward." (replied I.) We were immediately united by my Father, who tho' he had never taken orders had been bred to the Church.

Adeiu
Laura.

LETTER 7th
LAURA to MARIANNE

We remained but a few days after our Marriage, in the Vale of Uske. After taking an affecting Farewell of my Father, my Mother and my Isabel, I accompanied Edward to his Aunt's in Middlesex. Philippa received us both with every expression of affectionate Love. My arrival was indeed a most agreable surprise to her as she had not only been totally ignorant of my Marriage with her Nephew, but had never even had the slightest idea of there being such a person in the World.

Augusta, the sister of Edward was on a visit to her when we arrived. I found her exactly what her Brother had described her to be—of the middle size. She received me with equal surprise though not with equal Cordiality, as Philippa. There was a disagreable coldness and Forbidding Reserve in her reception of me which was equally distressing and Unexpected. None of that interesting Sensibility or amiable simpathy in her manners and Address to me when we first met which should have distinguished our introduction to each other. Her Language was neither warm, nor affectionate, her expressions of regard were neither animated nor cordial; her arms were not opened to receive me to her Heart, tho' my own were extended to press her to mine.

A short Conversation between Augusta and her Brother, which I accidentally overheard encreased my dislike to her, and convinced me that her Heart was no more formed for the soft ties of Love than for the endearing intercourse of Freindship.

"But do you think that my Father will ever be reconciled to this imprudent connection?" (said Augusta.)

"Augusta (replied the noble Youth) I thought you had a better opinion of me, than to imagine I would so abjectly degrade myself as to consider my Father's Concurrence in any of my affairs, either of Consequence or concern to me. Tell me Augusta tell me with sincerity; did you ever know me consult his inclinations or follow his Advice in the least trifling Particular since the age of fifteen?"

"Edward (replied she) you are surely too diffident in your own praise. Since you were fifteen only! My

Dear Brother since you were five years old, I entirely acquit you of ever having willingly contributed to the satisfaction of your Father. But still I am not without apprehensions of your being shortly obliged to degrade yourself in your own eyes by seeking a support for your wife in the Generosity of Sir Edward."

"Never, never Augusta will I so demean myself, (said Edward). Support! What support will Laura want which she can receive from him?"

"Only those very insignificant ones of Victuals and Drink." (answered she.)

"Victuals and Drink! (replied my Husband in a most nobly contemptuous Manner) and dost thou then imagine that there is no other support for an exalted mind (such as is my Laura's) than the mean and indelicate employment of Eating and Drinking?"

"None that I know of, so efficacious." (returned Augusta.)

"And did you then never feel the pleasing Pangs of Love, Augusta? (replied my Edward.) Does it appear impossible to your vile and corrupted Palate, to exist on Love? Can you not conceive the Luxury of living in every distress that Poverty can inflict, with the object of your tenderest affection?"

"You are too ridiculous (said Augusta) to argue with; perhaps however you may in time be convinced that . . ."

Here I was prevented from hearing the remainder of her speech, by the appearance of a very Handsome young Woman, who was ushured into the Room at the Door of which I had been listening. On hearing her announced by the Name of "Lady Dorothea," I instantly quitted my Post and followed her into the Parlour, for I well remembered that she was the Lady, proposed as a Wife for my Edward by the Cruel and Unrelenting Baronet.

Altho' Lady Dorothea's visit was nominally to Philippa and Augusta, yet I have some reason to imagine that (acquainted with the Marriage and arrival of Edward) to see me was a principal motive to it.

I soon perceived that tho' Lovely and Elegant in her Person and tho' Easy and Polite in her Address, she was of that inferior order of Beings with regard to Delicate Feeling, tender Sentiments, and refined Sensibility, of which Augusta was one.

She staid but half an hour and neither in the Course of her Visit, confided to me any of her secret thoughts, nor requested me to confide in her, any of Mine. You will easily imagine therefore my Dear Marianne that I could not feel any ardent affection or very sincere Attachment for Lady Dorothea.

Adeiu

Laura.

LETTER 8th

LAURA to MARIANNE, in continuation

Lady Dorothea had not left us long before another visitor as unexpected a one as her Ladyship, was announced. It was Sir Edward, who informed by Augusta of her Brother's marriage, came doubtless to reproach him for having dared to unite himself to me without his Knowledge. But Edward foreseeing his design, approached him with heroic fortitude as soon as he entered the Room, and addressed him in the following Manner.

"Sir Edward, I know the motive of your Journey here—You come with the base Design of reproaching me for having entered into an indissoluble engagement with my Laura without your Consent. But Sir, I glory in the Act—It is my greatest boast that I have incurred the displeasure of my Father!"

So saying, he took my hand and whilst Sir Edward, Philippa, and Augusta were doubtless reflecting with admiration on his undaunted Bravery, led me from the Parlour to his Father's Carriage which yet remained at the Door and in which we were instantly conveyed from the pursuit of Sir Edward.

The Postilions had at first received orders only to take the London road; as soon as we had sufficiently reflected However, we ordered them to Drive to

M——, the seat of Edward's most particular freind, which was but a few miles distant.

At M—— we arrived in a few hours; and on sending in our names were immediately admitted to Sophia, the Wife of Edward's freind. After having been deprived during the course of 3 weeks of a real freind (for such I term your Mother) imagine my transports at beholding one, most truly worthy of the Name. Sophia was rather above the middle size; most elegantly formed. A soft languor spread over her lovely features, but increased their Beauty—. It was the Charectarestic of her Mind—. She was all sensibility and Feeling. We flew into each others arms and after having exchanged vows of mutual Freindship for the rest of our Lives, instantly unfolded to each other the most inward secrets of our Hearts—. We were interrupted in the delightfull Employment by the entrance of Augustus, (Edward's freind) who was just returned from a solitary ramble.

Never did I see such an affecting Scene as was the meeting of Edward and Augustus.

"My Life! my Soul!" (exclaimed the former) "My adorable angel!" (replied the latter) as they flew into each other's arms. It was too pathetic for the feelings of Sophia and myself—We fainted alternately on a sofa.

Adeiu

Laura.

LETTER 9th

From the same to the same

Towards the close of the day we received the following Letter from Philippa.

"Sir Edward is greatly incensed by your abrupt departure; he has taken back Augusta with him to Bedfordshire. Much as I wish to enjoy again your charming society, I cannot determine to snatch you from that, of such dear and deserving Freinds— When your Visit to them is terminated, I trust you will return to the arms of your

"Philippa."

We returned a suitable answer to this affectionate Note and after thanking her for her kind invitation assured her that we would certainly avail ourselves of it, whenever we might have no other place to go to. Tho' certainly nothing could to any reasonable Being, have appeared more satisfactory, than so gratefull a reply to her invitation, yet I know not how it was, but she was certainly capricious enough to be displeased with our behaviour and in a few weeks after, either to revenge our Conduct, or releive her own solitude, married a young and illiterate Fortune-hunter. This imprudent step (tho' we were sensible that it would probably deprive us of that fortune which Philippa had ever taught us to expect) could not on our own accounts, excite from our exalted minds a single sigh; yet fearfull lest it might prove a source of endless misery to the deluded Bride, our trembling Sensibility was greatly affected when we were first informed of the Event. The affectionate Entreaties of Augustus and Sophia that we would for ever consider their House as our Home, easily prevailed on us to determine never more to leave them. In the society of my Edward and this Amiable Pair, I passed the happiest moments of my Life; Our time was most delightfully spent in mutual Protestations of Freindship, and in vows of unalterable Love, in which we were secure from being interrupted, by intruding and disagreable Visitors, as Augustus and Sophia had on their first Entrance in the Neighbourhood, taken due care to inform the surrounding Families, that as their Happiness centered wholly in themselves, they wished for no other society. But alas! my Dear Marianne such Happiness as I then enjoyed was too perfect to be lasting. A most severe and unexpected Blow at once destroyed every sensation of Pleasure. Convinced as you must be from what I have already told you concerning Augustus and Sophia, that there never were a happier Couple, I need not, I imagine, inform you that their union had been contrary to the inclinations of their Cruel and Mercenery Parents; who had vainly endeavoured with obstinate

Perseverance to force them into a Marriage with those whom they had ever abhorred; but with an Heroic Fortitude worthy to be related and admired, they had both constantly refused to submit to such despotic Power.

After having so nobly disentangled themselves from the shackles of Parental Authority, by a Clandestine Marriage, they were determined never to forfeit the good opinion they had gained in the World, in so doing, by accepting any proposals of reconciliation that might be offered them by their Fathers—to this farther tryal of their noble independance however they never were exposed.

They had been married but a few months when our visit to them commenced during which time they had been amply supported by a considerable sum of money which Augustus had gracefully purloined from his unworthy father's Escritoire, a few days before his union with Sophia.

By our arrival their Expenses were considerably encreased tho' their means for supplying them were then nearly exhausted. But they, Exalted Creatures! scorned to reflect a moment on their pecuniary Distresses and would have blushed at the idea of paying their Debts.—Alas! what was their Reward for such disinterested Behaviour! The beautifull Augustus was arrested and we were all undone. Such perfidious Treachery in the merciless perpetrators of the Deed will shock your gentle nature Dearest Marianne as much as it then affected the Delicate sensibility of Edward, Sophia, your Laura, and of Augustus himself. To compleat such un-paralelled Barbarity we were informed that an Execution in the House would shortly take place. Ah! what could we do but what we did! We sighed and fainted on the sofa.

Adeiu

Laura.

LETTER 10th

LAURA in continuation

When we were somewhat recovered from the overpowering Effusions of our grief, Edward desired that we would consider what was the most prudent step to be taken in our unhappy situation while he repaired to his imprisoned freind to lament over his misfortunes. We promised that we would, and he set forwards on his journey to Town. During his absence we faithfully complied with his Desire and after the most mature Deliberation, at length agreed that the best thing we could do was to leave the House; of which we every moment expected the officers of Justice to take possession. We waited therefore with the greatest impatience, for the return of Edward in order to impart to him the result of our Deliberations. But no Edward appeared. In vain did we count the tedious moments of his absence—in vain did we weep—in vain even did we sigh—no Edward returned—. This was too cruel, too unexpected a Blow to our Gentle Sensibility—we could not support it—we could only faint. At length collecting all the Resolution I was Mistress of, I arose and after packing up some necessary apparel for Sophia and myself, I dragged her to a Carriage I had ordered and we instantly set out for London. As the Habitation of Augustus was within twelve miles of Town, it was not long e'er we arrived there, and no sooner had we entered Holboun than letting down one of the Front Glasses I enquired of every decent-looking Person that we passed "If they had seen my Edward?"

But as we drove too rapidly to allow them to answer my repeated Enquiries, I gained little, or indeed, no information concerning him. "Where am I to Drive?" said the Postilion. "To Newgate Gentle Youth (replied I), to see Augustus." "Oh! no, no, (exclaimed Sophia) I cannot go to Newgate; I shall not be able to support the sight of my Augustus in so cruel a confinement—my feelings are sufficiently shocked by the *recital*, of his Distress, but to behold it will overpower my Sensibility." As I perfectly agreed with her in the Justice of her Sentiments the Postilion was instantly directed to return into the Country. You may perhaps have been somewhat surprised my Dearest Marianne, that in the Distress I then endured, destitute of any support, and unprovided with any Habitation, I should never once have remembered my Father and Mother or my paternal Cottage in the Vale of Uske. To account for the seeming forgetfullness I must inform you of a trifling circumstance concerning them which I have as yet never mentioned. The death of my Parents a few weeks after my Departure, is the circumstance I allude to. By their decease I became the lawfull Inheritress of their House and Fortune. But alas! the House had never been their own and their Fortune had only been an Annuity on their own Lives. Such is the Depravity of the World! To your Mother I should have returned with Pleasure, should have been happy to have introduced to her, my charming Sophia and should with Chearfullness have passed the remainder of my Life in their dear Society in the Vale of Uske, had not one obstacle to the execution of so agreable a scheme, intervened; which was the Marriage and Removal of your Mother to a distant part of Ireland.

Adeiu

Laura.

LETTER 11th

LAURA in continuation

"I have a Relation in Scotland (said Sophia to me as we left London) who I am certain would not hesitate in receiving me." "Shall I order the Boy to drive there?" said I—but instantly recollecting myself, exclaimed, "Alas I fear it will be too long a Journey for the Horses." Unwilling however to act only from my own inadequate Knowledge of the Strength and Abilities of Horses, I consulted the Postilion, who was entirely of my Opinion concerning the Affair. We therefore determined to change Horses at the next Town and to travel Post the remainder of the Journey—. When we arrived at the last Inn we were to stop at, which was but a few miles from the House of Sophia's Relation, unwilling to intrude our Society on him unexpected and unthought of, we wrote a very elegant and well penned Note to him containing an account of our Destitute and melancholy Situation, and of our intention to spend some months with him in Scotland. As soon as we had dispatched this Letter, we immediately prepared to follow it in person and were stepping into the Carriage for that Purpose when our attention was attracted by the Entrance of a coroneted Coach and 4 into the Inn-yard. A Gentleman considerably advanced in years, descended from it. At his first

Appearance my Sensibility was wonderfully affected and e'er I had gazed at him a 2^d time, an instinctive sympathy whispered to my Heart, that he was my Grandfather. Convinced that I could not be mistaken in my conjecture I instantly sprang from the Carriage I had just entered, and following the Venerable Stranger into the Room he had been shewn to, I threw myself on my knees before him and besought him to acknowledge me as his Grand Child. He started, and after having attentively examined my features, raised me from the Ground and throwing his Grandfatherly arms around my Neck, exclaimed, "Acknowledge thee! Yes dear resemblance of my Laurina and Laurina's Daughter, sweet image of my Claudia and my Claudia's Mother, I do acknowledge thee as the Daughter of the one and the Grandaughter of the other." While he was thus tenderly embracing me, Sophia astonished at my precipitate Departure, entered the Room in search of me. No sooner had she caught the eye of the venerable Peer, than he exclaimed with every mark of astonishment—"Another Grandaughter! Yes, yes, I see you are the Daughter of my Laurina's eldest Girl; Your resemblance to the beauteous Matilda sufficiently proclaims it." "Oh!" replied Sophia, "when I first beheld you the instinct of Nature whispered me that we were in some degree related—But whether Grandfathers, or Grandmothers, I could not pretend to determine." He folded her in his arms, and whilst they were tenderly embracing, the Door of the Apartment opened and a most beautifull young Man appeared. On perceiving him Lord St. Clair started and retreating back a few paces, with uplifted Hands, said, "Another Grand-child! What an unexpected Happiness is this! to discover in the space of 3 minutes, as many of my Descendants! This, I am certain is Philander the son of my Laurina's 3d girl the amiable Bertha; there wants now but the presence of Gustavus to compleat the Union of my Laurina's Grand-Children."

"And here he is; (said a Gracefull Youth who that instant entered the room) here is the Gustavus you desire to see. I am the son of Agatha your Laurina's 4th and youngest Daughter." "I see you are indeed;" replied Lord St. Clair—"But tell me (continued he looking fearfully towards the Door) tell me, have I any other Grand-children in the House." "None my Lord." "Then I will provide for you all without farther delay—Here are 4 Banknotes of 50£ each—Take them and remember I have done the Duty of a Grandfather." He instantly left the Room and immediately afterwards the House.

Adeiu

Laura.

LETTER the 12th

LAURA in continuation

You may imagine how greatly we were surprised by the sudden departure of Lord St. Clair. "Ignoble Grand-sire!" exclaimed Sophia. "Unworthy Grandfather!" said I, and instantly fainted in each other's arms. How long we remained in this situation I know not; but when we recovered we found ourselves alone, without either Gustavus, Philander, or the Banknotes. As we were deploring our unhappy fate, the Door of the Apartment opened and "Macdonald" was announced. He was Sophia's cousin. The haste with which he came to our releif so soon after the receipt of our Note, spoke so greatly in his favour that I hesitated not to pronounce him at first sight, a tender and simpathetic Freind. Alas! he little deserved the name—for though he told us that he was much concerned at our Misfortunes, yet by his own account it appeared that the perusal of them, had neither drawn from him a single sigh, nor induced him to bestow one curse on our vindictive stars—. He told Sophia that his Daughter depended on her returning with him to Macdonald-Hall, and that as his Cousin's freind he should be happy to see me there also. To Macdonald-Hall, therefore we went, and were received with great kindness by Janetta the Daughter of Macdonald, and the Mistress of the Mansion. Janetta was then only fifteen; naturally well disposed, endowed with a susceptible Heart, and a simpathetic Disposition, she might, had these amiable qualities been properly encouraged, have been an ornament to human Nature; but unfortunately her Father possessed not a soul sufficiently exalted to admire so promising a Disposition, and had endeavoured by every means in his power to prevent its encreasing with her Years. He had actually so far extinguished the natural noble Sensibility of her Heart, as to prevail on her to accept an offer from a young Man of his Recommendation. They were to be married in a few months, and Graham, was in the House when we arrived. *We* soon saw through his character. He was just such a Man as one might have expected to be the choice of Macdonald. They said he was Sensible, well-informed, and Agreable; we did not pretend to Judge of such trifles, but as we were convinced he had no soul, that he had never read the sorrows of Werter, and that his Hair bore not the least resemblance to auburn, we were certain that Janetta could feel no affection for him, or at least that she ought to feel none. The very circumstance of his being her father's choice too, was so much in his disfavour, that had he been deserving her, in every other respect yet *that* of itself ought to have been a sufficient reason in the Eyes of Janetta for rejecting him.

These considerations we were determined to represent to her in their proper light and doubted not of meeting with the desired success from one naturally so well disposed; whose errors in the affair had only arisen from a want of proper confidence in her own opinion, and a suitable contempt of her father's. We found her indeed all that our warmest wishes could have hoped for; we had no difficulty to convince her that it was impossible she could love Graham, or that it was her Duty to disobey her Father; the only thing at which she rather seemed to hesitate was our assertion that she must be attached to some other Person. For some time, she persevered in declaring that she knew no other young man for whom she had the smallest Affection; but upon explaining the impossibility of such a thing she said that she beleived she *did like* Captain M'Kenrie better than any one she knew besides. This confession satisfied us and after having enumerated the good Qualities of M'Kenrie and assured her that she was violently in love with him, we desired to know whether he had ever in any wise declared his affection to her.

"So far from having ever declared it, I have no reason to imagine that he has ever felt any for me." said Janetta. "That he certainly adores you (replied Sophia) there can be no doubt—. The Attachment must be reciprocal. Did he never gaze on you with

27

admiration—tenderly press your hand—drop an involantary tear—and leave the room abruptly?" "Never (replied she) that I remember—he has always left the room indeed when his visit has been ended, but has never gone away particularly abruptly or without making a bow." Indeed my Love (said I) you must be mistaken—for it is absolutely impossible that he should ever have left you but with Confusion, Despair, and Precipitation. Consider but for a moment Janetta, and you must be convinced how absurd it is to suppose that he could ever make a Bow, or behave like any other Person." Having settled this Point to our satisfaction, the next we took into consideration was, to determine in what manner we should inform M'Kenrie of the favourable Opinion Janetta entertained of him . . . We at length agreed to acquaint him with it by an anonymous Letter which Sophia drew up in the following manner.

"Oh! happy Lover of the beautifull Janetta, oh! amiable Possessor of *her* Heart whose hand is destined to another, why do you thus delay a confession of your attachment to the amiable Object of it? Oh! consider that a few weeks will at once put an end to every flattering Hope that you may now entertain, by uniting the unfortunate Victim of her father's Cruelty to the execrable and detested Graham.

"Alas! why do you thus so cruelly connive at the projected Misery of her and of yourself by delaying to communicate that scheme which had doubtless long possessed your imagination? A secret Union will at once secure the felicity of both."

The amiable M'Kenrie, whose modesty as he afterwards assured us had been the only reason of his having so long concealed the violence of his affection for Janetta, on receiving this Billet flew on the wings of Love to Macdonald-Hall, and so powerfully pleaded his Attachment to her who inspired it, that after a few more private interveiws, Sophia and I experienced the satisfaction of seeing them depart for Gretna-Green, which they chose for the celebration of their Nuptials, in preference to any other place although it was at a considerable distance from Macdonald-Hall.

Adeiu

Laura.

LETTER the 13th

LAURA in continuation

They had been gone nearly a couple of Hours, before either Macdonald or Graham had entertained any suspicion of the affair. And they might not even then have suspected it, but for the following little Accident. Sophia happening one day to open a private Drawer in Macdonald's Library with one of her own keys, discovered that it was the Place where he kept his Papers of consequence and amongst them some bank notes of considerable amount. This discovery she imparted to me; and having agreed together that it would be a proper treatment of so vile a Wretch as Macdonald to deprive him of money, perhaps dishonestly gained, it was determined that the next time we should either of us happen to go that way, we would take one or more of the Bank notes from the drawer. This well meant Plan we had often successfully put in Execution; but alas! on the very day of Janetta's Escape, as Sophia was majestically removing the 5th Bank-note from the Drawer to her own purse, she was suddenly most impertinently interrupted in her employment by the entrance of Macdonald himself, in a most abrupt and precipitate Manner. Sophia (who though naturally all winning sweetness could when occasions demanded it call forth the Dignity of her sex) instantly put on a most forbiding look, and darting an angry frown on the undaunted culprit, demanded in a haughty tone of voice "Wherefore her retirement was thus insolently broken in on?" The unblushing Macdonald, without even endeavouring to exculpate himself from the crime he was charged with, meanly endeavoured to reproach Sophia with ignobly defrauding him of his money . . . The dignity of Sophia was wounded; "Wretch (exclaimed she, hastily replacing the Bank-note in the Drawer) how darest thou to accuse me of an Act, of which the bare idea makes me blush?" The base wretch was still unconvinced and continued to upbraid the justly-offended Sophia in such opprobious Language, that at length he so greatly provoked the gentle sweetness of her Nature, as to induce her to revenge herself on him by informing him of Janetta's Elopement, and of the active Part we had both taken in the affair. At this period of their Quarrel I entered the Library and was as you may imagine equally offended as Sophia at the ill-grounded accusations of the malevolent and contemptible Macdonald. "Base Miscreant! (cried I) how canst thou thus undauntedly endeavour to sully the spotless reputation of such bright Excellence? Why dost thou not suspect *my* innocence as soon?" "Be satisfied Madam (replied he) I *do* suspect it, and therefore must desire that you will both leave this House in less than half an hour."

"We shall go willingly; (answered Sophia) our hearts have long detested thee, and nothing but our freindship for thy Daughter could have induced us to remain so long beneath thy roof."

"Your Freindship for my Daughter has indeed

been most powerfully exerted by throwing her into the arms of an unprincipled Fortune-hunter." (replied he.)

"Yes, (exclaimed I) amidst every misfortune, it will afford us some consolation to reflect that by this one act of Freindship to Janetta, we have amply discharged every obligation that we have received from her father."

"It must indeed be a most gratefull reflection, to your exalted minds." (said he.)

As soon as we had packed up our wardrobe and valuables, we left Macdonald Hall, and after having walked about a mile and a half we sate down by the side of a clear limpid stream to refresh our exhausted limbs. The place was suited to meditation. A grove of full-grown Elms sheltered us from the East—. A Bed of full-grown Nettles from the West—. Before us ran the murmuring brook and behind us ran the turn-pike road. We were in a mood for contemplation and in a Disposition to enjoy so beautifull a spot. A mutual silence which had for some time reigned between us, was at length broke by my exclaiming—"What a lovely scene! Alas why are not Edward and Augustus here to enjoy its Beauties with us?"

"Ah! my beloved Laura (cried Sophia) for pity's sake forbear recalling to my remembrance the unhappy situation of my imprisoned Husband. Alas, what would I not give to learn the fate of my Augustus! to know if he is still in Newgate, or if he is yet hung. But never shall I be able so far to conquer my tender sensibility as to enquire after him. Oh! do not I beseech you ever let me again hear you repeat his beloved name—. It affects me too deeply—. I cannot bear to hear him mentioned it wounds my feelings."

"Excuse me my Sophia for having thus unwillingly offended you—" replied I—and then changing the conversation, desired her to admire the noble Grandeur of the Elms which sheltered us from the Eastern Zephyr. "Alas! my Laura (returned she) avoid so melancholy a subject, I intreat you. Do not again wound my Sensibility by observations on those elms. They remind me of Augustus. He was like them, tall, magestic—he possessed that noble grandeur which you admire in them."

I was silent, fearfull lest I might any more unwillingly distress her by fixing on any other subject of conversation which might again remind her of Augustus.

"Why do you not speak my Laura? (said she after a short pause) "I cannot support this silence you must not leave me to my own reflections; they ever recur to Augustus."

"What a beautifull sky! (said I) How charmingly

is the azure varied by those delicate streaks of white!"

"Oh! my Laura (replied she hastily withdrawing her Eyes from a momentary glance at the sky) do not thus distress me by calling my Attention to an object which so cruelly reminds me of my Augustus's blue sattin waistcoat striped with white! In pity to your unhappy freind avoid a subject so distressing." What could I do? The feelings of Sophia were at that time so exquisite, and the tenderness she felt for Augustus so poignant that I had not power to start any other topic, justly fearing that it might in some unforseen manner again awaken all her sensibility by directing her thoughts to her Husband. Yet to be silent would be cruel; she had intreated me to talk.

From this Dilemma I was most fortunately releived by an accident truly apropos; it was the lucky overturning of a Gentleman's Phaeton, on the road which ran murmuring behind us. It was a most fortunate accident as it diverted the attention of Sophia from the melancholy reflections which she had been before indulging. We instantly quitted our seats and ran to the rescue of those who but a few moments before had been in so elevated a situation as a fashionably high Phaeton, but who were now laid low and sprawling in the Dust. "What an ample subject for reflection on the uncertain Enjoyments of this World, would not that Phaeton and the Life of Cardinal Wolsey afford a thinking Mind!" said I to Sophia as we were hastening to the field of Action.

She had not time to answer me, for every thought was now engaged by the horrid spectacle before us. Two Gentlemen most elegantly attired but weltering in their blood was what first struck our Eyes—we approached—they were Edward and Augustus—. Yes dearest Marianne they were our Husbands. Sophia shrieked and fainted on the ground—I screamed and instantly ran mad—. We remained thus mutually deprived of our senses, some minutes, and on regaining them were deprived of them again. For an Hour and a Quarter did we continue in this unfortunate situation—Sophia fainting every moment and I running mad as often. At length a groan from the hapless Edward (who alone retained any share of life) restored us to ourselves. Had we indeed before imagined that either of them lived, we should have been more sparing of our Greif—but as we had supposed when we first beheld them that they were no more, we knew that nothing could remain to be done but what we were about. No sooner therefore did we hear my Edward's groan than postponing our lamentations for the present, we hastily ran to the Dear Youth and kneeling on each side of him implored him not to die—. "Laura (said He fixing his now languid Eyes on me) I fear I have been overturned."

I was overjoyed to find him yet sensible.

"Oh! tell me Edward (said I) tell me I beseech you before you die, what has befallen you since that unhappy Day in which Augustus was arrested and we were separated—"

"I will" (said he) and instantly fetching a deep sigh, Expired—. Sophia immediately sunk again into a swoon—. *My* greif was more audible. My Voice faltered, My Eyes assumed a vacant stare, my face became as pale as Death, and my senses were considerably impaired—.

"Talk not to me of Phaetons (said I, raving in a frantic, incoherent manner)—Give me a violin—. I'll play to him and sooth him in his melancholy Hours—Beware ye gentle Nymphs of Cupid's Thunderbolts, avoid the piercing shafts of Jupiter—Look at that grove of Firs—I see a Leg of Mutton—They told me Edward was not Dead; but they deceived me—they took him for a cucumber—" Thus I continued wildly exclaiming on my Edward's Death—. For two Hours did I rave thus madly and should not then have left off, as I was not in the least fatigued, had not Sophia who was just recovered from her swoon, intreated me to consider that Night was now approaching and that the Damps began to fall. "And whither shall we go (said I) to shelter us from either?" "To that white Cottage." (replied she pointing to a neat Building which rose up amidst the grove of Elms and which I had not before observed—) I agreed and we instantly walked to it—we knocked at the door—it was opened by an old woman; on being requested to afford us a Night's Lodging, she informed us that her House was but small, that she had only two Bedrooms, but that However we should be wellcome to one of them. We were satisfied and followed the good woman into the House where we were greatly cheered by the sight of a comfortable fire—. She was a Widow and had only one Daughter, who was then just seventeen—One of the best of ages; but alas! she was very plain and her name was Bridget . . . Nothing therefore could be expected from her—she could not be supposed to possess either exalted Ideas, Delicate Feelings or refined Sensibilities—. She was nothing more than a mere good-tempered, civil and obliging young woman; as such we could scarcely dislike her—she was only an Object of Contempt—.

Adeiu

Laura.

LETTER the 14th

LAURA in continuation

Arm yourself my amiable young Freind with all the philosophy you are Mistress of; summon up all the fortitude you possess, for alas! in the perusal of the following Pages your sensibility will be most severely tried. Ah! what were the misfortunes I had before experienced and which I have already related to you, to the one I am now going to inform you of. The Death of my Father, my Mother, and my Husband though almost more than my gentle Nature could support, were trifles in comparison to the misfortune I am now proceeding to relate. The morning after our arrival at the Cottage, Sophia complained of a violent pain in her delicate limbs, accompanied with a disagreable Head-ake. She attributed it to a cold caught by her continued faintings in the open air as the Dew was falling the Evening before. That I feared was but too probably the case; since how could it be otherwise accounted for that I should have escaped the same indisposition, but by supposing that the bodily Exertions I had undergone in my repeated fits of frenzy had so effectually circulated and warmed my Blood as to make me proof against the chilling Damps of Night, whereas, Sophia lying totally inactive on the ground must have been exposed to all their severity. I was most seriously

38

alarmed by her illness which trifling as it may appear to you, a certain instinctive sensibility whispered me, would in the End be fatal to her.

Alas! my fears were but too fully justified; she grew gradually worse—and I daily became more alarmed for her. At length she was obliged to confine herself solely to the Bed allotted us by our worthy Landlady—. Her disorder turned to a galloping Consumption and in a few days carried her off. Amidst all my Lamentations for her (and violent you may suppose they were) I yet received some consolation in the reflection of my having paid every attention to her, that could be offered, in her illness. I had wept over her every Day—had bathed her sweet face with my tears and had pressed her fair Hands continually in mine—. "My beloved Laura (said she to me a few Hours before she died) take warning from my unhappy End and avoid the imprudent conduct which had occasioned it . . . Beware of fainting-fits . . . Though at the time they may be refreshing and agreable yet beleive me they will in the end, if too often repeated and at improper seasons, prove destructive to your Constitution . . . My fate will teach you this . . . I die a Martyr to my greif for the loss of Augustus . . . One fatal swoon has cost me my Life . . . Beware of swoons Dear Laura . . . A frenzy fit is not one quarter so pernicious; it is an exercise to the Body and if not too violent, is I dare say conducive to Health in its consequences—Run mad as often as you chuse; but do not faint—"

These were the last words she ever addressed to me . . . It was her dieing Advice to her afflicted Laura, who has ever most faithfully adhered to it.

After having attended my lamented freind to her Early Grave, I immediately (tho' late at night) left the detested Village in which she died, and near which had expired my Husband and Augustus. I had not walked many yards from it before I was overtaken by a stage-coach, in which I instantly took a place, determined to proceed in it to Edinburgh, where I hoped to find some kind some pitying Freind who would receive and comfort me in my afflictions.

It was so dark when I entered the Coach that I could not distinguish the Number of my Fellow-travellers; I could only perceive that they were many. Regardless however of anything concerning them, I gave myself up to my own sad Reflections. A general silence prevailed—A silence, which was by nothing interrupted but by the loud and repeated snores of one of the Party.

"What an illiterate villain must that man be! (thought I to myself) What a total want of delicate refinement must he have, who can thus shock our senses by such a brutal noise! He must I am certain be capable of every bad action! There is no crime too black for such a Character!" Thus reasoned I within myself, and doubtless such were the reflections of my fellow travellers.

At length, returning Day enabled me to behold the unprincipled Scoundrel who had so violently disturbed my feelings. It was Sir Edward the father of my Deceased Husband. By his side, sate Augusta, and on the same seat with me were your Mother and Lady Dorothea. Imagine my surprise at finding myself thus seated amongst my old Acquaintance. Great as was my astonishment, it was yet increased, when on looking out of Windows, I beheld the Husband of Philippa, with Philippa by his side, on the Coachbox and when on looking behind I beheld, Philander and Gustavus in the Basket. "Oh! Heavens, (exclaimed I) is it possible that I should so unexpectedly be surrounded by my nearest Relations and Connections?" These words roused the rest of the Party, and every eye was directed to the corner in which I sat. "Oh! my Isabel (continued I throwing myself across Lady Dorothea into her arms) receive once more to your Bosom the unfortunate Laura. Alas! when we last parted in the Vale of Usk, I was happy in being united to the best of Edwards; I had then a Father and a Mother, and had never known misfortunes—But now deprived of every freind but you—"

"What! (interrupted Augusta) is my Brother dead then? Tell us I intreat you what is become of him?" "Yes, cold and insensible Nymph, (replied I) that luckless swain your Brother, is no more, and you may now glory in being the Heiress of Sir Edward's fortune."

Although I had always despised her from the Day I had overheard her conversation with my Edward, yet in civility I complied with hers and Sir Edward's intreaties that I would inform them of the whole melancholy affair. They were greatly shocked—even the obdurate Heart of Sir Edward and the insensible one of Augusta, were touched with sorrow, by the unhappy tale. At the request of your Mother I related to them every other misfortune which had befallen me since we parted. Of the imprisonment of Augustus and the absence of Edward—of our arrival in Scotland—of our unexpected Meeting with our Grand-father and our cousins—of our visit to Macdonald-Hall—of the singular service we there performed towards Janetta—of her Fathers ingratitude for it . . . of his inhuman Behaviour, unaccountable suspicions, and barbarous treatment of us, in obliging us to leave the House . . . of our lamentations on the loss of Edward and Augustus and finally of the melancholy Death of my beloved Companion.

Pity and surprise were strongly depictured in your Mother's countenance, during the whole of my narration, but I am sorry to say, that to the eternal reproach of her sensibility, the latter infinitely predominated. Nay, faultless as my conduct had certainly been during the whole course of my late misfortunes and adventures, she pretended to find fault with my behaviour in many of the situations in which I had been placed. As I was sensible myself, that I had always behaved in a manner which reflected Honour on my Feelings and Refinement, I paid little attention to what she said, and desired her to satisfy my Curiosity by informing me how she came there, instead of wounding my spotless reputation with unjustifiable Reproaches. As soon as she had complied with my wishes in this particular and had given me an accurate detail of every thing that had befallen her since our separation (the particulars of which if you are not already acquainted with, your Mother will give you) I applied to Augusta for the same information respecting herself, Sir Edward and Lady Dorothea.

She told me that having a considerable taste for the Beauties of Nature, her curiosity to behold the delightful scenes it exhibited in that part of the

World had been so much raised by Gilpin's Tour to the Highlands, that she had prevailed on her Father to undertake a Tour to Scotland and had persuaded Lady Dorothea to accompany them. That they had arrived at Edinburgh a few Days before and from thence had made daily Excursions into the Country around in the Stage Coach they were then in, from one of which Excursions they were at that time returning. My next enquiries were concerning Philippa and her Husband, the latter of whom I learned having spent all her fortune, had recourse for subsistence to the talent in which, he had always most excelled, namely, Driving, and that having sold every thing which belonged to them except their Coach, had converted it into a Stage and in order to be removed from any of his former Acquaintance, had driven it to Edinburgh from whence he went to Sterling every other Day. That Philippa still retaining her affection for her ungratefull Husband, had followed him to Scotland and generally accompanied him in his little Excursions to Sterling. "It has only been to throw a little money into their Pockets (continued Augusta) that my Father has always travelled in their Coach to veiw the beauties of the Country since our arrival in Scotland—for it would certainly have been much more agreable to us, to visit the Highlands in a Postchaise than merely to travel from Edinburgh to Sterling and from Sterling to Edinburgh every other Day in a crowded and uncomfortable Stage." I perfectly agreed with her in her sentiments on the affair, and secretly blamed Sir Edward for thus sacrificing his Daughter's Pleasure for the sake of a ridiculous old woman whose folly in marrying so young a man ought to be punished. His Behaviour however was entirely of a peice with his general Character; for what could be expected from a man who possessed not the smallest atom of Sensibility, who scarcely knew the meaning of simpathy, and who actually snored—.

Adeiu

Laura.

LETTER the 15th
LAURA in continuation
When we arrived at the town where we were to Breakfast, I was determined to speak with Philander and Gustavus, and to that purpose as soon as I left the Carriage, I went to the Basket and tenderly enquired after their Health, expressing my fears of the uneasiness of their situation. At first they seemed rather confused at my appearance dreading no doubt that I might call them to account for the money which our Grandfather had left me and which they had unjustly deprived me of, but finding that I mentioned

nothing of the Matter, they desired me to step into the Basket as we might there converse with greater ease. Accordingly I entered and whilst the rest of the party were devouring green tea and buttered toast, we feasted ourselves in a more refined and sentimental Manner by a confidential Conversation. I informed them of every thing which had befallen me during the course of my life, and at my request they related to me every incident of theirs.

"We are the sons as you already know, of the two youngest Daughters which Lord St. Clair had by Laurina an Italian opera girl. Our mothers could neither of them exactly ascertain who were our Father, though it is generally beleived that Philander, is the son of one Philip Jones a Bricklayer and that my Father was Gregory Staves a Staymaker of Edinburgh. This is however of little consequence for as our Mothers were certainly never married to either of them it reflects no Dishonour on our Blood, which is of a most ancient and unpolluted kind. Bertha (the Mother of Philander) and Agatha (my own Mother) always lived together. They were neither of them very rich; their united fortunes had originally amounted to nine thousand Pounds, but as they had always lived upon the principal of it, when we were fifteen it was diminished to nine Hundred. This nine Hundred, they always kept in a

Drawer in one of the Tables which stood in our common sitting Parlour, for the convenience of having it always at Hand. Whether it was from this circumstance, of its being easily taken, or from a wish of being independant, or from an excess of sensibility (for which we were always remarkable) I cannot now determine, but certain it is that when we had reached our 15th year, we took the nine Hundred Pounds and ran away. Having obtained this prize we were determined to manage it with eoconomy and not to spend it either with folly or Extravagance. To this purpose we therefore divided it into nine parcels, one of which we devoted to Victuals, the 2^d to Drink, the 3^d to Housekeeping, the 4th to Carriages, the 5th to Horses, the 6th to Servants, the 7th to Amusements the 8th to Cloathes and the 9th to Silver Buckles. Having thus arranged our Expences for two months (for we expected to make the nine Hundred Pounds last as long) we hastened to London and had the good luck to spend it in 7 weeks and a Day which was 6 Days sooner than we had intended. As soon as we had thus happily disencumbered ourselves from the weight of so much money, we began to think of returning to our Mothers, but accidentally hearing that they were both starved to Death, we gave over the design and determined to engage ourselves to some strolling

47

Company of Players, as we had always a turn for the Stage. Accordingly we offered our services to one and were accepted; our Company was indeed rather small, as it consisted only of the Manager his wife and ourselves, but there were fewer to pay and the only inconvenience attending it was the Scarcity of Plays which for want of People to fill the Characters, we could perform. We did not mind trifles however—. One of our most admired Performances was *Macbeth*, in which we were truly great. The Manager always played *Banquo* himself, his Wife my *Lady Macbeth*. I did the *Three Witches* and Philander acted *all the rest*. To say the truth this tragedy was not only the Best, but the only Play we ever performed; and after having acted it all over England, and Wales, we came to Scotland to exhibit it over the remainder of Great Britain. We happened to be quartered in that very Town, where you came and met your Grandfather—. We were in the Inn-yard when his Carriage entered and perceiving by the arms to whom it belonged, and knowing that Lord St. Clair was our Grandfather, we agreed to endeavour to get something from him by discovering the Relationship—. You know how well it succeeded—. Having obtained the two Hundred Pounds, we instantly left the Town, leaving our Manager and his Wife to act *Macbeth* by themselves, and took the road to Sterling, where we spent our little fortune with great *eclat*. We are now returning to Edinburgh in order to get some preferment in the Acting way; and such my Dear Cousin is our History."

I thanked the amiable Youth for his entertaining narration, and after expressing my wishes for their Welfare and Happiness, left them in their little Habitation and returned to my other Freinds who impatiently expected me.

My adventures are now drawing to a close my dearest Marianne; at least for the present.

When we arrived at Edinburgh Sir Edward told me that as the Widow of his son, he desired I would accept from his Hands of four Hundred a year. I graciously promised that I would, but could not help observing that the unsimpathetic Baronet offered it more on account of my being the Widow of Edward than in being the refined and amiable Laura.

I took up my Residence in a romantic Village in the Highlands of Scotland where I have ever since continued, and where I can uninterrupted by unmeaning Visits, indulge in a melancholy solitude, my unceasing Lamentations for the Death of my Father, my Mother, my Husband and my Freind.

Augusta has been for several years united to Graham the Man of all others most suited to her; she became acquainted with him during her stay in Scotland.

Sir Edward in hopes of gaining an Heir to his Title and Estate, at the same time married Lady Dorothea—. His wishes have been answered.

Philander and Gustavus, after having raised their reputation by their Performances in the Theatrical Line at Edinburgh, removed to Covent Garden, where they still Exhibit under the assumed names of *Luvis* and *Quick*.

Philippa has long paid the Debt of Nature, Her Husband however still continues to drive the Stage-Coach from Edinburgh to Sterling:—

Adeiu my Dearest Marianne.

Laura.

Finis
June 13th 1790.

Ƈ

FRANCIS BACON
1561–1626

Bacon received a classical education, first from his
Puritan mother and English Crown officer father,
and then, from the age of twelve, as a scholar at
Cambridge University. He became a barrister and
politician, progressing to solicitor-general, attorney-
general, lord keeper and, in 1618, lord chancellor.
Convicted of taking bribes, in 1621 he was imprisoned in the Tower of London, a disgrace that
ended his public life. By then he had already appeared in print and penned the *Novum Organum*, an
aphoristic Latin treatise intended to demonstrate
humanity's subordination of nature. During the last
five years of his life, he wrote most vigorously, ex-
tending knowledge of the natural world and pursuing classification of the sciences. 'Of Friendship',
the essay reprinted here, reflects both Bacon's pro-
fessional life at court and his classificatory zeal. He
compares the fruits of friendship to the many-
kernelled pomegranate, focusing on three of its
diplomatically useful parts: that it brings peace to
our affections, aids good judgement, and supports
our worldly actions.

'Of Friendship'

It had been hard for him that spake it, to have put more truth and untruth together in few words, than in that Speech, *Whosoever is delighted in solitude, is either a wilde Beast, or a God.* For it is most true, that a natural and secret hatred, and aversation towards *Society* in any Man, hath somewhat of the savage Beast; but it is most untrue, that it should have any character at all of the Divine Nature, except it proceed not out of a pleasure in *Solitude*, but out of a love and desire to sequester a man's self for a higher conversation; such as is found to have been falsely and feignedly in some of the Heathen, as *Epimenides* the *Candian*, *Numa* the *Roman*, *Empedocles* the *Sicilian*, and *Apollonius* of *Tyana*; and truly and really in divers of the ancient Hermits, and Holy Fathers of the Church. But little do men perceive what *Solitude* is, and how far it extendeth: for a Crowd is not Company, and Faces are but a Gallery of Pictures, and Talk but a *Tinckling Cymbal*, where there is no *Love*. The Latine Adage meeteth with it a little, *Magna Civitas, magna solitudo*; because in a great Town *Friends* are scattered, so that there is not that fellowship, for the most part, which is in less *Neighborhoods*. But we may go further, and affirm most truly, that it is a mere and miserable *solitude* to want true *Friends*, without which the World is but a Wilderness: and even in this Sense also of *Solitude*, whosoever in the Frame of his nature and Affections is unfit for *Friendship*, he taketh it of the Beast, and not from Humanity.

A Principal *Fruit* of *Friendship* is, the Ease and Discharge of the Fulness and Swellings of the Heart, which Passions of all kinds do cause and induce. We know Diseases of Stoppings and Suffocations are the most dangerous in the Body, and it is not much otherwise in the Mind; You may take *Sarza* to open the Liver, *Steel* to open the Spleen, *Flower* of *Sulphur* for the Lungs, *Castoreum* for the Brain; but no Receipt openeth the Heart, but a true Friend, to whom you may impart Griefs, Joys, Fears, Hopes, Suspicions, Counsels, and whatsoever lieth upon the Heart, to oppress it, in a kind of Civil Shrift or Confession.

It is a strange thing to observe, how high a Rate Great Kings and Monarchs do set upon this *Fruit* of *Friendship* wherof we speak; so great, as they purchase it many times at the hazard of their own Safety and Greatness. For Princes, in regard of the distance of their Fortune from that of their Subjects and Servants, cannot gather this *Fruit* except (to make Themselves capable thereof) they raise some Persons to be as it were Companions, and almost Equals to themselves, which many times sorteth to Inconvenience. The modern Languages give unto such Persons the name of *Favorites* or *Privadoes*, as if it were matter of Grace or Conversation. But the *Roman* name attaineth the true Use and Cause thereof, naming them *Participes Curarum*; for it is that which tyeth the knot. And we see plainly that this hath been done, not by weak and Passionate *Princes* only, but by the Wisest, and most Politique that ever reigned: Who have oftentimes joyned to themselves some of their Servants, whom both themselves have called *Friends*, and allowed others likewise to call them in the same manner, using the word which is received between private men.

L. Sylla, when he commanded *Rome* raised *Pompey* (after surnamed the *Great*) to that Height, that *Pompey* vaunted himself for *Sylla's* Overmatch: for when he had carried the *Consulship* for a Friend of his against the pursuit of *Sylla*, and that *Sylla* did a little resent thereat, and began to speak great, *Pompey* turned upon him again, and in effect bade him be quiet; *For that more men adored the Sun rising, than the Sun setting.* With *Julius Cæsar*, *Decimus Brutus* had obtained that Interest, as he set him down in his Testament, for Heir in Remainder after his *Nephew*. And this was the Man that had power with him, to draw him forth to his death. For when

Cæsar would have discharged the Senate, in regard of some ill presages, and specially a Dream of *Calpurnia*; This Man lifted him gently by the Arm out of his Chair, telling him, he hoped he would not dismiss the Senate, till his Wife had dreamt a better Dream. And it seemeth his favour was so great, as *Antonius* in a Letter which is recited *Verbatim* in one of *Cicero's Philippiques*, calleth him *Venefica, Witch*; as if he had enchanted *Cæsar*. *Augustus* raised *Agrippa* (though of mean Birth) to that Height, as when he consulted with *Mæcenas* about the Marriage of his Daughter *Julia, Mæcenas* took the Liberty to tell him, *That he must either marry his Daughter to* Agrippa, *or take away his life, there was no third way, he had made him so great*. With *Tiberius Cæsar, Sejanus* had ascended to that Height, as they two were tearmed and reckoned as a pair of Friends. *Tiberius* in a Letter to him, saith, *Hæc pro Amicitia nostra non occultavi*; and the whole Senate dedicated an Altar to *Friendship*, as to a *Goddess*, in respect of the great Dearness of *Friendship* between them two. The like or more was between *Septimius Severus* and *Plautianus*: for he forced his eldest Son to marry the Daughter of *Plautianus*, and would often maintain *Plautianus* in doing affronts to his Son, and did write also in a Letter to the Senate by these words; *I love the Man so well, as I wish he may over-live me*. Now if these Princes had been as a *Trajan*, or a *Marcus Aurelius*, a Man might have thought, that this had proceeded of an abundant Goodness of Nature; but being men so Wise, of such strength and severity of Mind, and so extream Lovers of themselves, as all these were; it proveth most plainly, that they found their own Felicity (though as great as ever happened to mortal men) but as an half Piece, except they mought have a *Friend* to make it Entire; and yet, which is more, they were *Princes* that had Wives, Sons, Nephews, and yet all these could not supply the Comfort of *Friendship*.

It is not to be forgotten, what *Commineus* observeth of his first Master, *Duke Charles* the *Hardy*; namely, That he would communicate his Secrets with none; and least of all those Secrets which troubled him most. Whereupon he goeth on, and saith, that towards his latter time; *That closeness did impair, and a little perish his understanding.* Surely, *Commineus* might have made the same Judgment also, if it had pleased him, of his second Master, *Lewis* the Eleventh, whose Closeness was indeed his Tormentor. The Parable of *Pythagoras* is dark, but true, *Cor ne edito, Eat not the Heart.* Certainly, if a man would give it a hard Phrase, those that want *Friends* to open themselves unto, are Cannibals of their own *Hearts.* But one thing is most admirable, (wherewith I will conclude this first *Fruit* of *Friendship*) which is, That this Communicating of a Man's Self to his *Friend*, works two contrary Effects; for it redoubleth Joyes and cutteth *Griefs* in Halfs; for there is no man that imparteth his *Joyes* to his *Friend*, but he *Joyeth* the more; and no man that imparteth his *Griefs* to his *Friend*, but he *grieveth* the less. So that it is, in truth of Operation upon a Man's Mind, of like vertue, as the *Alchymists* used to attribute to their Stone for Man's Body, that it worketh all contrary Effects, but still to the Good and Benefit of Nature; but yet, without praying in Aid of *Alchymists*, there is a manifest Image of this in the ordinary course of Nature: for in Bodies, *Union* strengthneth and cherisheth any natural Action; and on the other side, weakneth and dulleth any violent Impression; and even so it is of Minds.

The second *Fruit* of *Friendship* is Healthfull and Sovereign for the *Understanding*, as the first is for the Affections: for *Friendship* maketh indeed a *fair Day* in the *Affections* from Storm and Tempests; but it maketh *Day-light* in the *Understanding* out of Darkness and Confusion of Thoughts. Neither is this to be understood only of Faithful Counsel which a man receiveth from his *Friend*: but before you come to that, certain it is, that whosoever hath his Mind fraught with many Thoughts, his Wits and understanding do clarifie and break up in the Communicating and Discoursing with another; He tosseth his Thoughts more easily, He marshalleth them more orderly, He seeth how they look when they are turned into words. Finally, He waxeth Wiser than Himself; and that more by an Hour's Discourse, than by a Day's Meditation. It was well said by *Themistocles* to the King of *Persia*; *That Speech was like Cloth of Arras opened and put abroad*; *whereby the Imagery doth appear in Figure, whereas in Thoughts they lye but as in Packs*. Neither is this second *Fruit* of *Friendship*, in opening the *Understanding*, restrained only to such *Friends* as are able to give a man Counsel; (they indeed are best) but even without that a man learneth of himself, and bringeth his own Thoughts to Light, and whetteth his Wits as against a Stone, which itself cuts not. In a word, a Man were better relate himself to a Statue or Picture, than to suffer his Thoughts to pass in smother.

Add now, to make this second *Fruit* of *Friendship* compleat, that other Point which lyeth more open, and falleth within Vulgar Observation, which is *Faithful Counsel* from a *Friend*. *Heraclitus* saith well in one of his Ænigmaes; *Dry light is ever the best*. And certain it is, that the Light that a man receiveth by *Counsel* from another, is dryer and purer than that which cometh from his own *Understanding* and *Judg-*

ment, which is ever infused and drenched in his *Affections* and *Customs*. So as, there is as much difference between the *Counsel* that a *Friend* giveth, and that a man giveth himself, as there is between the *Counsel* of a *Friend*, and of a *Flatterer*: For there is no such *Flatterer*, as is a man's self; and there is no such remedy against *Flattery* of a man's self, as the Liberty of a *Friend*. *Counsel* is of two sorts; the one concerning *Manners*, the other concerning *Business*. For the first; The best preservative to keep the Mind in Health, is the faithfull Admonition of a *Friend*. The calling of a man's Self to a strict Account, is a Medicine sometimes too Piercing and Corrosive. Reading good Books of *Morality*, is a little Flat and Dead. Observing our Faults in Others, is sometimes unproper for our Case. But the best Receipt (best (I say) to work, and best to take) is the Admonition of a *Friend*. It is a strange thing to behold, what gross Errours, and extream Absurdities, many (especially of the greater Sort) do commit, for want of a *Friend* to tell them of them, to the great damage both of their Fame and Fortune: for, as *S. James* saith, they are as Men *that look sometimes into a Glass, and presently forget their own Shape and Favor.* As for *Business*, a Man may think, if he will, that two Eyes see no more than one; or that a Gamester seeth always more than a Looker on; or that a man in Anger is as wise as he that hath said over the four and twenty Letters; or that a Musket may be shot off as well upon the Arm, as upon a Rest; and such other fond and high Imaginations, to think himself All in All. But when all is done, the help of good *Counsel* is that which setteth *Business* straight; and if any man think, that he will take *Counsel*, but it shall be by pieces, asking *Counsel* in one business of one man, and in another business of another man; It is well, (that is to say, better perhaps than if he asked none at all) but he runneth two dangers; One, that he shall not be faithfully counselled; for it is a rare thing, except it be from a perfect and entire *Friend*, to have *Counsel* given, but such as shall be bowed and crooked to some ends, which he hath that giveth it. The other, that he shall have *Counsel* given, hurtful, and unsafe, (though with good meaning) and mixt; partly of mischief, and partly of remedy: even as if you would call a Physician, that is thought good, for the Cure of the Disease you complain of, but is unacquainted with your Body; and therefore may put you in a way for a present Cure, but overthroweth your Health in some other kind, and so cure the Disease, and kill the Patient. But a *Friend*, that is wholly acquainted with a man's Estate, will beware, by furthering any present *Business*, how he dasheth upon other Inconvenience. And therefore rest not upon *scattered*

Counsels; they will rather distract and mis-lead, than settle and direct.

After these two noble *Fruits* of *Friendship*, (*Peace in the Affections*, and *Support of the Judgment*) followeth the last *Fruit* which is like the *Pomegranate*, full of many kernells; I mean *Aid*, and *Bearing a Part* in all *Actions* and *Occasions*. Here the best way to represent to life the manifold use of *Friendship*, is to cast and see, how many things there are, which a man cannot do himself; and then it will appear, that it was a sparing Speech of the Ancients, to say, *That a Friend is another himself*; for that a *Friend* is far more than *himself*. Men have their time, and die many times in desire of some things, which they principally take to *heart*; The bestowing of a Child, the finishing of a Work, or the like. If a man have a true *Friend*, he may rest almost secure, that the care of those things will continue after him: So that a man hath as it were two Lives in his desires. A man hath a Body, and that Body is confined to a place; but where *Friendship* is, all Offices of Life are as it were granted to him, and his Deputy: for he may exercise them by his *Friend*. How many things are there, which a man cannot with any face or comeliness, say or do himself? A man can scarce alledge his own merits with modesty, much less extoll them: A man cannot sometimes brook to supplicate or beg;

and a number of the like. But all these things are graceful in a *friend's* mouth, which are blushing in a man's own. So again, a man's Person hath many proper Relations, which he cannot put off. A man cannot speak to his Son, but as a Father; to his Wife, but as a Husband; to his Enemy, but upon tearms: Whereas a *Friend* may speak, as the Case requires, and not as it sorteth with the Person. But to enumerate these things were endless: I have given the Rule, where a man cannot fitly play his own part: If he have not a *Friend*, he may quit the Stage.

JAMES BOSWELL
1740–1795

Born in Scotland and trained as a lawyer, Boswell courted the attention of Europe's major figures – including Rousseau, Voltaire and, most importantly, the English man of letters Samuel Johnson – to fulfil his wish to join the world of Enlightenment politics and letters. In London, he joined the Club, a celebrated tap-room congregation of leading figures, including Johnson, Oliver Goldsmith, Edmund Burke and Adam Smith. Boswell insists in *The Life of Samuel Johnson*, his compendious account of his friend, that 'the feeling of friendship is like that of being comfortably filled with roast beef; love, like being enlivened with champagne'. As the excerpt that follows shows, the gifted Dr Johnson instantly picks up on Boswell's unattributed paraphrase from Edmund Waller's seventeenth-century poem 'To Amoret' and vigorously disagrees. This is typical of the spotlight Boswell threw on the genius of his more famous associate and travelling companion (see his *Journal of a Tour of the Hebrides*). Boswell spent the last decade of his life in the colossal task of encompassing Johnson in print.

from *The Life of Samuel Johnson*

On Friday, April 10, I dined with him at General Oglethorpe's, where we found Dr. Goldsmith. [. . .] A question was started, how far people who disagree in a capital point can live in friendship together. Johnson said they might. Goldsmith said they could not, as they had not the *idem velle atque idem nolle*— the same likings and the same aversions. JOHNSON. 'Why, Sir, you must shun the subject as to which you disagree. For instance, I can live very well with Burke: I love his knowledge, his genius, his diffusion, and affluence of conversation; but I would not talk to him of the Rockingham party.' GOLDSMITH. 'But, Sir, when people live together who have something as to which they disagree, and which they want to shun, they will be in the situation mentioned in the story of Bluebeard: "You may look into all the chambers but one." But we should have the greatest inclination to look into that chamber, to talk of that subject.' JOHNSON. (with a loud voice,) 'Sir, I am not saying that *you* could live in friendship with a man from whom you differ as to some point: I am only saying that *I* could do it. You put me in mind of Sappho in Ovid.'

[. . .] On Sunday, April 16, being Easter Day, after having attended the solemn service at St. Paul's, I dined with Dr. Johnson and Mrs. Williams. I maintained that Horace was wrong in placing happiness in *Nil admirari*, for that I thought admiration one of the most agreeable of all our feelings; and I regretted that I had lost much of my disposition to admire, which people generally do as they advance in life. JOHNSON. 'Sir, as a man advances in life, he gets what is better than admiration—judgement, to estimate things at their true value.' I still insisted that admiration was more pleasing than judgement, as love is more pleasing than friendship. The feeling of friendship is like that of being comfortably filled with roast beef; love, like being enlivened with champagne. JOHNSON. 'No, Sir; admiration and love are like being intoxicated with champagne; judgement and friendship like being enlivened. Waller has hit upon the same thought with you: but I don't believe you have borrowed from Waller. I wish you would enable yourself to borrow more.'

❦

RALPH WALDO EMERSON
1803–1882

Philosopher, poet, essayist, pastor and lecturer – all of Emerson's endeavours served to shape his notion of Transcendentalism, an optimistic mid-nineteenth-century mystic idealism advocating communion with nature and privileged moments of intellectual insight. Emerson's intense focus on private experience, self-reliance and solitude proved difficult to reconcile with sociability. Prolonged discussions about the nature of friendship with fellow New England thinkers Margaret Fuller and Henry David Thoreau enabled Emerson to arrive at the compromise he describes in 'Friendship', which follows here. No friendship is perfect, he warns, and he who holds out for his ideal may walk alone for a long time. 'All association must be a compromise,' he writes. The essay's central paradox is that a friend can help you discover a better version of yourself, but you need to do the actual work of becoming a better person on your own.

'Friendship'

We have a great deal more kindness than is ever spoken. Maugre all the selfishness that chills like east winds the world, the whole human family is bathed with an element of love like a fine ether. How many persons we meet in houses, whom we scarcely speak to, whom yet we honour, and who honour us! How many we see in the street, or sit with in church, whom, though silently, we warmly rejoice to be with! Read the language of these wandering eye-beams. The heart knoweth.

The effect of the indulgence of this human affection is a certain cordial exhilaration. In poetry, and in common speech, the emotions of benevolence and complacency which are felt towards others, are likened to the material effects of fire; so swift, or much more swift, more active, more cheering, are these fine inward irradiations. From the highest degree of passionate love, to the lowest degree of good will, they make the sweetness of life.

Our intellectual and active powers increase with our affection. The scholar sits down to write, and all his years of meditation do not furnish him with one good thought or happy expression; but it is necessary to write a letter to a friend—and, forthwith, troops of gentle thoughts invest themselves, on every hand, with chosen words. See in any house where virtue and self-respect abide, the palpitation which the approach of a stranger causes. A commended stranger is expected and announced, and an uneasiness betwixt pleasure and pain invades all the hearts of a household. His arrival almost brings fear to the good hearts that would welcome him. The house is dusted, all things fly into their places, the old coat is exchanged for the new, and they must get up a dinner if they can. Of a commended stranger, only the good report is told by others, only the good and new is heard by us. He stands to us for humanity. He is what we wish. Having imagined and invested him, we ask how we should stand related in conversation and action with such a man, and are uneasy with fear. The same idea exalts conversation with him. We talk better than we are wont. We have the nimblest fancy, a richer memory, and our dumb devil has taken leave for the time. For long hours we can continue a series of sincere, graceful, rich communications, drawn from the oldest, secretest experience, so that they who sit by, of our own kinsfolk and acquaintance, shall feel a lively surprise at our unusual powers. But as soon as the stranger begins to intrude his partialities, his definitions, his defects, into the conversation, it is all over. He has heard the first, the last, and best he will ever hear from us. He is no stranger now. Vulgarity, ignorance, misapprehension, are old acquaintances. Now, when he comes, he may get the order, the dress, and the dinner—but the throbbing of the heart, and the communications of the soul, no more.

Pleasant are these jets of affection which relume a young world for me again. Delicious is a just and firm encounter of two, in a thought, in a feeling. How beautiful, on their approach to this beating heart, the steps and forms of the gifted and the true! The moment we indulge our affections, the earth is metamorphosed: there is no winter, and no night: all tragedies, all ennuis vanish; all duties even; nothing fills the proceeding eternity but the forms all radiant of beloved persons. Let the soul be assured that somewhere in the universe it should rejoin its friend, and it would be content and cheerful alone for a thousand years.

I awoke this morning with devout thanksgiving for my friends, the old and the new. Shall I not call God the Beautiful, who daily showeth himself so to me in his gifts? I chide society, I embrace solitude, and yet I am not so ungrateful as not to see the wise, the lovely, and the noble-minded, as from time to time they pass my gate. Who hears me, who understands me, becomes mine—a possession for all time. Nor is nature so poor, but she gives me this joy several times, and thus we weave social threads of our own, a new web of relations; and, as many thoughts in succession substantiate themselves, we shall by and by stand in a new world of our own creation, and no longer strangers and pilgrims in a traditionary globe. My friends have come to me unsought. The great God gave them to me. By oldest right, by the divine affinity of virtue with itself, I find them, or rather, not I, but the Deity in me and in them, both deride and cancel the thick walls of individual character, relation, age, sex, and circumstance, at which he usually connives, and now makes many one. High thanks I owe you, excellent lovers, who carry out the world for me to new and noble depths, and enlarge the meaning of all my thoughts. These are not stark and stiffened persons, but the new-born poetry of God—poetry without stop—hymn, ode, and epic, poetry still flowing, and not yet caked in dead books with annotation and grammar, but Apollo and the Muses chanting still. Will these too separate themselves from me again, or some of them? I know not, but I fear it not; for my relation to them is so pure, that we hold by simple affinity, and the Genius of my life being thus social, the same affinity will exert its energy on whomsoever is as noble as these men and women, wherever I may be.

I confess to an extreme tenderness of nature on

this point. It is almost dangerous to me to "crush the sweet poison of misused wine" of the affections. A new person is to me always a great event, and hinders me from sleep. I have had such fine fancies lately about two or three persons, as have given me delicious hours; but the joy ends in the day; it yields no fruit. Thought is not born of it; my action is very little modified. I must feel pride in my friend's accomplishments as if they were mine—wild, delicate, throbbing property in his virtues. I feel as warmly when he is praised, as the lover when he hears applause of his engaged maiden. We overestimate the conscience of our friend. His goodness seems better than our goodness, his nature finer, his temptations less. Everything that is his, his name, his form, his dress, his books and instruments, fancy enhances. Our own thought sounds new and larger from his mouth.

Yet the systole and diastole of the heart are not without their analogy in the ebb and flow of love. Friendship, like the immortality of the soul, is too good to be believed. The lover, beholding his maiden, half knows that she is not verily that which he worships; and in the golden hour of friendship we are surprised with shades of suspicion and unbelief. We doubt that we bestow on our hero the virtues in which he shines, and afterwards worship the form to which we have ascribed this divine inhabitation. In strictness, the soul does not respect men as it respects itself. In strict science, all persons underlie the same condition of an infinite remoteness. Shall we fear to cool our love by facing the fact, by mining for the metaphysical foundation of this Elysian temple? Shall I not be as real as the things I see? If I am, I shall not fear to know them for what they are. Their essence is not less beautiful than their appearance, though it needs finer organs for its apprehension. The root of the plant is not unsightly to science, though for chaplets and festoons we cut the stem short. And I must hazard the production of the bald fact amidst these pleasing reveries, though it should prove an Egyptian skull at our banquet. A man who stands united with his thought, conceives magnificently of himself. He is conscious of a universal success, even though bought by uniform particular failures. No advantages, no powers, no gold or force can be any match for him. I cannot choose but rely on my own poverty, more than on your wealth. I cannot make your consciousness tantamount to mine. Only the star dazzles; the planet has a faint, moon-like ray. I hear what you say of the admirable parts and tried temper of the party you praise, but I see well that for all his purple cloaks I shall not like him, unless he is at last a poor Greek like me. I cannot deny it, O friend, that the vast shadow of the Phenomenal includes thee, also, in its pied and painted immensity—thee, also, compared with whom all else is shadow. Thou art not Being, as Truth is, as Justice is—thou art not my soul, but a picture and effigy of that. Thou hast come to me lately, and already thou art seizing thy hat and cloak. Is it not that the soul puts forth friends, as the tree puts forth leaves, and presently, by the germination of new buds, extrudes the old leaf? The law of nature is alternation for evermore. Each electrical state superinduces the opposite. The soul environs itself with friends, that it may enter into a grander self-acquaintance or solitude; and it goes alone, for a season, that it may exalt its conversation or society. This method betrays itself along the whole history of our personal relations. Ever the instinct of affection revives the hope of union with our mates, and ever the returning sense of insulation recalls us from the chase. Thus every man passes his life in the search after friendship; and if he should record his true sentiment, he might write a letter like this, to each new candidate for his love:—

DEAR FRIEND,

If I was sure of thee, sure of thy capacity, sure to match my mood with thine, I should never think again of trifles, in relation to thy comings and goings. I am not very wise: my moods are quite attainable: and I respect thy genius; it is to me as yet unfathomed; yet dare I not presume in thee a perfect intelligence of me, and so thou art to me a delicious torment. Thine ever, or never.

Yet these uneasy pleasures and fine pains are for curiosity, and not for life. They are not to be indulged. This is to weave cobweb, and not cloth. Our friendships hurry to short and poor conclusions, because we have made them a texture of wine and dreams, instead of the tough fibre of the human heart. The laws of friendship are great, austere, and eternal, of one web with the laws of nature and of morals. But we have aimed at a swift and petty benefit, to suck a sudden sweetness. We snatch at the slowest fruit in the whole garden of God, which many summers and many winters must ripen. We seek our friend not sacredly, but with an adulterate passion which would appropriate him to ourselves. In vain. We are armed all over with subtle antagonisms, which, as soon as we meet, begin to play, and translate all poetry into stale prose. Almost all people descend to meet. All association must be a compromise, and, what is worst, the very flower and aroma of the flower of each of the beautiful natures disappears as they approach each other. What a perpetual disappointment is actual society, even of the virtuous and gifted! After interviews have been compassed with long foresight, we must be tormented presently by baffled blows, by sudden, unseasonable apathies, by epilepsies of wit and of animal spirits, in the heyday of friendship and thought. Our faculties do not play us true, and both parties are relieved by solitude.

I ought to be equal to every relation. It makes no difference how many friends I have, and what content I can find in conversing with each, if there be one to whom I am not equal. If I have shrunk unequal from one contest, instantly the joy I find in all the rest becomes mean and cowardly. I should hate myself, if then I made my other friends my asylum.

> "The valiant warrior famoused for fight,
> After a hundred victories, once foiled,
> Is from the book of honour razed quite,
> And all the rest forgot for which he toiled."

Our impatience is thus sharply rebuked. Bashfulness and apathy are a tough husk in which a delicate organization is protected from premature ripening. It would be lost if it knew itself before any of the best souls were yet ripe enough to know and own it.

Respect the *naturlangsamkeit* which hardens the ruby in a million years, and works in duration, in which Alps and Andes come and go as rainbows. The good spirit of our life has no heaven which is the price of rashness. Love, which is the essence of God, is not for levity, but for the total worth of man. Let us not have this childish luxury in our regards; but the austerest worth; let us approach our friend with an audacious trust in the truth of his heart, in the breadth, impossible to be overturned, of his foundations.

The attractions of this subject are not to be resisted; and I leave, for the time, all account of subordinate social benefit, to speak of that select and sacred relation which is a kind of absolute, and which even leaves the language of love suspicious and common, so much is this purer, and nothing is so much divine.

I do not wish to treat friendships daintily, but with roughest courage. When they are real, they are not glass threads or frost-work, but the solidest thing we know. For now, after so many ages of experience, what do we know of nature, or of ourselves? Not one step has man taken toward the solution of the problem of his destiny. In one condemnation of folly stand the whole universe of men. But the sweet sincerity of joy and peace, which I draw from this alliance with my brother's soul, is the nut itself whereof all nature and all thought is but the husk and shell. Happy is the house that shelters a friend. It might well be built, like a festal bower or arch, to entertain him a single day. Happier, if he know the solemnity of that relation, and honour its law. It is no idle band, no holiday engagement. He who offers himself a candidate for that covenant, comes up, like an Olympian, to the great games, where the first-born of the world are the competitors. He proposes himself for contests where Time, Want, Danger are in the lists, and he alone is victor who has truth enough in his constitution to preserve the delicacy of his beauty from the wear and tear of all these. The gifts of fortune may be present or absent, but all the hap in that contest depends on intrinsic nobleness, and the contempt of trifles. There are two elements that go to the composition of friendship, each so sovereign, that I can detect no superiority in either, no reason why either should be first named. One is Truth. A friend is a person with whom I may be sincere. Before him, I may think aloud. I am arrived at last in the presence of a man so real and equal, that I may drop even those undermost garments of dissimulation, courtesy, and second thought, which men never put off, and may deal with him with the simplicity and wholeness with which one chemical

77

atom meets another. Sincerity is the luxury allowed, like diadems and authority, only to the highest rank, *that* being permitted to speak truth, as having none above it to court or conform unto. Every man alone is sincere. At the entrance of a second person, hypocrisy begins. We parry and fend the approach of our fellow-man by compliments, by gossip, by amusements, by affairs. We cover up our thought from him under a hundred folds. I knew a man who, under a certain religious frenzy, cast off this drapery, and omitting all compliment and common-place, spoke to the conscience of every person he encountered, and that with great insight and beauty. At first he was resisted, and all men agreed he was mad. But persisting, as indeed he could not help doing, for some time in this course, he attained to the advantage of bringing every man of his acquaintance into true relations with him. No man would think of speaking falsely with him, or of putting him off with any chat of markets or reading-rooms. But every man was constrained by so much sincerity to face him; and what love of nature, what poetry, what symbol of truth he had, he did certainly show him. But to most of us society shows not its face and eye, but its side and its back. To stand in true relations with men in a false age, is worth a fit of insanity, is it not? We can seldom go erect. Almost every man we meet requires some civility, requires to be humoured; he has some fame, some talent, some whim of religion or philanthropy in his head that is not to be questioned, and so spoils all conversation with him. But a friend is a sane man who exercises not my ingenuity, but me. My friend gives me entertainment without requiring me to stoop, or to lisp, or to mask myself. A friend, therefore, is a sort of paradox in nature. I who alone am, I who see nothing in nature whose existence I can affirm with equal evidence to my own, behold now the semblance of my being in all its height, variety, and curiosity, reiterated in a foreign form; so that a friend may well be reckoned the masterpiece of nature.

The other element of friendship is Tenderness. We are holden to men by every sort of tie, by blood, by pride, by fear, by hope, by lucre, by lust, by hate, by admiration, by every circumstance and badge and trifle, but we can scarce believe that so much character can subsist in another as to draw us by love. Can another be so blessed, and we so pure, that we can offer him tenderness? When a man becomes dear to me, I have touched the goal of fortune. I find very little written directly to the heart of this matter in books. And yet I have one text which I cannot choose but remember. My author says, "I offer myself faintly and bluntly to those whose I effectually am, and tender myself least to him to whom I am the most devoted." I wish that friendship should have feet, as well as eyes and eloquence. It must plant itself on the ground, before it walks over the moon. I wish it to be a little of a citizen, before it is quite a cherub. We chide the citizen because he makes love a commodity. It is an exchange of gifts, of useful loans; it is good neighbourhood; it watches with the sick; it holds the pall at the funeral; and quite loses sight of the delicacies and nobility of the relation. But though we cannot find the god under this disguise of a sutler, yet, on the other hand, we cannot forgive the poet if he spins his thread too fine, and does not substantiate his romance by the municipal virtues of justice, punctuality, fidelity, and pity. I hate the prostitution of the name of friendship to signify modish and worldly alliances. I much prefer the company of ploughboys and tin-pedlars, to the silken and perfumed amity which only celebrates its days of encounter by a frivolous display, by rides in a curricle, and dinners at the best taverns. The end of friendship is a commerce the most strict and homely that can be joined; more strict than any of which we have experience. It is for aid and comfort through all the relations and passages of life and death. It is fit for serene days, and graceful gifts, and country rambles, but also for rough roads and hard fare, shipwreck, poverty, and persecution. It keeps company with the sallies of the wit and the trances of religion. We are to dignify to each other the daily needs and offices of man's life, and embellish it by courage, wisdom, and unity. It should never fall into something usual and settled, but should be alert and inventive, and add rhyme and reason to what was drudgery.

For perfect friendship it may be said to require natures so rare and costly, so well tempered each, and so happily adapted, and withal so circumstanced, (for even in that particular, a poet says, love demands that the parties be altogether paired,) that very seldom can its satisfaction be realized. It cannot subsist in its perfection, say some of those who are learned in this warm lore of the heart, betwixt more than two. I am not quite so strict in my terms, perhaps because I have never known so high a fellowship as others. I please my imagination more with a circle of godlike men and women variously related to each other, and between whom subsists a lofty intelligence. But I find this law of *one to one*, peremptory for conversation, which is the practice and consummation of friendship. Do not mix waters too much. The best mix as ill as good and bad. You shall have very useful and cheering discourse at several times with two several men, but let all three of you come together, and you shall not have one new and hearty word. Two may talk and one may hear, but three cannot take part in a conversation of the most sincere and searching sort. In good company there is never such discourse between two, across the table, as takes place when you leave them alone. In good company, the individuals at once merge their egotism into a social soul exactly co-extensive with the several consciousnesses there present. No partialities of friend to friend, no fondnesses of brother to sister, of wife to husband, are there pertinent, but quite otherwise. Only he may then speak who can sail on the common thought of the party, and not poorly limited to his own. Now this convention, which good sense demands, destroys the high freedom of great conversation, which requires an absolute running of two souls into one.

No two men but being left alone with each other, enter into simpler relations. Yet it is affinity that determines *which* two shall converse. Unrelated men give little joy to each other; will never suspect the latent powers of each. We talk sometimes of a great talent for conversation, as if it were a permanent property in some individuals. Conversation is an evanescent relation—no more. A man is reputed to have thought and eloquence : he cannot, for all that, say a word to his cousin or his uncle. They accuse his silence with as much reason as they would blame the insignificance of a dial in the shade. In the sun it will mark the hour. Among those who enjoy his thought, he will regain his tongue.

Friendship requires that rare mean betwixt likeness and unlikeness, that piques each with the presence of power and of consent in the other party. Let me be alone to the end of the world, rather than that my friend should overstep by a word or a look his real sympathy. I am equally baulked by antagonism and by compliance. Let him not cease an instant to be himself. The only joy I have in his being mine, is that the *not mine* is *mine*. It turns the stomach, it blots the daylight; where I looked for a manly furtherance, or at least a manly resistance, to find a mush of concession. Better be a nettle in the side of your friend than his echo. The condition which high friendship demands, is ability to do without it. To be capable of that high office, requires great and sublime parts. There must be very two, before there can be very one. Let it be an alliance of two large formidable natures, mutually beheld, mutually feared, before yet they recognise the deep identity which beneath these disparities unites them.

He only is fit for this society who is magnanimous. He must be so, to know its law. He must be one who is sure that greatness and goodness are always economy. He must be one who is not swift to intermeddle with his fortunes. Let him not dare to intermeddle with this. Leave to the diamond its ages to grow, nor expect to accelerate the births of the eternal. Friendship demands a religious treatment. We must not be wilful, we must not provide. We talk of choosing our friends, but friends are self-elected. Reverence is a great part of it. Treat your friend as a spectacle. Of course, if he be a man, he has merits that are not yours, and that you cannot honour, if you must needs hold him close to your person. Stand aside. Give those merits room. Let them mount and expand. Be not so much his friend that you can never know his peculiar energies, like fond mammas who shut up their boy in the house until he is almost grown a girl. Are you the friend of your friend's buttons, or of his thought? To a great heart he will still be a stranger in a thousand particulars, that he may come near in the holiest ground. Leave it to girls and boys to regard a friend as property, and to suck a short and all-confounding pleasure instead of the pure nectar of God.

Let us buy our entrance to this guild by a long probation. Why should we desecrate noble and beautiful souls by intruding on them? Why insist on rash personal relations with your friend? Why go to his house, or know his mother and brother and sisters? Why be visited by him at your own? Are these things material to our covenant? Leave this touching and clawing. Let him be to me a spirit. A message, a thought, a sincerity, a glance from him, I want, but not news, nor pottage. I can get politics, and chat, and neighbourly conveniences, from cheaper companions. Should not the society of my friend be to me poetic, pure, universal, and great as nature itself? Ought I to feel that our tie is profane in comparison with yonder bar of cloud that sleeps on the horizon, or that clump of waving grass that divides the brook? Let us not vilify, but raise it to that standard. That great defying eye, that scornful beauty of his mien and action, do not pique yourself on reducing, but rather fortify and enhance. Worship his superiorities. Wish him not less by a thought, but hoard and tell them all. Guard him as thy great counterpart; have a princedom to thy friend. Let him be to thee for ever a sort of beautiful enemy, untameable, devoutly revered, and not a trivial conveniency to be soon outgrown and cast aside. The hues of the opal, the light of the diamond, are not to be seen if the eye is too near. To my friend I write a letter, and from him I receive a letter. That seems to you a little. Me it suffices. It is a spiritual gift worthy of him to give, and of me to receive. It profanes nobody. In these warm lines the heart will trust itself, as it will not to the tongue, and pour out the prophecy of a godlier existence than all the annals of heroism have yet made good.

Respect so far the holy laws of this fellowship as not to prejudice its perfect flower by your impatience for its opening. We must be our own, before we can be another's. There is at least this satisfaction in crime, according to the Latin Proverb; you can speak to your accomplice on even terms. *Crimen quos inquinat, aequat.* To those whom we admire and love, at first we cannot. Yet the least defect of self-possession vitiates, in my judgment, the entire relation. There can never be deep peace between two spirits, never mutual respect, until, in their dialogue, each stands for the whole world.

What is so great as friendship, let us carry with what grandeur of spirit we can. Let us be silent—so we may hear the whisper of the gods. Let us not interfere. Who set you to cast about what you should say to the select souls, or to say anything to such? No matter how ingenious, no matter how graceful and bland. There are innumerable degrees of folly and wisdom, and for you to say aught is to be frivolous. Wait, and thy soul shall speak. Wait until the necessary and everlasting overpowers you, until day and night avail themselves of your lips. The only money of God, is God. He pays never with anything less, or anything else. The only reward of virtue, is virtue: the only way to have a friend, is to be one. Vain to hope to come nearer a man by getting into his house. If unlike, his soul only flees the faster from you, and you shall catch never a true glance of his eye. We see the noble afar off, and they repel us; why should we intrude? Late—very late—we perceive that no arrangements, no introductions, no consuetudes or habits of society, would be of any avail to establish us in such relations with them as we desire—but solely the uprise of nature in us to the same degree it is in them: then shall we meet as water with water; and if we should not meet them then, we shall not want them, for we are already they. In the last analysis, love is only the reflection of a man's own worthiness from other men. Men have sometimes exchanged names with their friends, as if they would signify that in their friend each loved his own soul.

The higher the style we demand of friendship, of course the less easy to establish it with flesh and blood. We walk alone in the world. Friends, such as we desire, are dreams and fables. But a sublime hope cheers ever the faithful heart, that elsewhere, in other regions of the universal power, souls are now acting, enduring, and daring, which can love us, and which we can love. We may congratulate ourselves that the period of nonage, of follies, of blunders, and of shame, is passed in solitude, and when we are finished men, we shall grasp heroic hands in heroic hands. Only be admonished by what you already see, not to strike leagues of friendship with cheap persons, where no friendship can be. Our impatience betrays us into rash and foolish alliances which no God attends. By persisting in your path, though you forfeit the little, you gain the great. You become pronounced. You demonstrate yourself, so as to put yourself out of the reach of false relations, and you draw to you the first-born of the world—those rare pilgrims whereof only one or two wander in nature at once, and before whom the vulgar great, show as spectres and shadows merely.

It is foolish to be afraid of making our ties too spiritual, as if so we could lose any genuine love. Whatever correction of our popular views we make from insight, nature will be sure to bear us out in, and though it seem to rob us of some joy, will repay us with a greater. Let us feel, if we will, the absolute insulation of man. We are sure that we have all in us. We go to Europe, or we pursue persons, or we read books, in the instinctive faith that these will call it out, and reveal us to ourselves. Beggars all. The persons are such as we; the Europe, an old faded garment of dead persons; the books, their ghosts

Let us drop this idolatry. Let us give over this mendicancy. Let us even bid our dearest friends farewell, and defy them, saying, "Who are you? Unhand me: I will be dependent no more." Ah! seest thou not, O brother, that thus we part only to meet again on a higher platform, and only be more each other's because we are more our own? A friend is Janus-faced: he looks to the past and the future. He is the child of all my foregoing hours, the prophet of those to come. He is the harbinger of a greater friend. It is the property of the divine to be reproductive.

I do then with my friends as I do with my books. I would have them where I can find them, but I seldom use them. We must have society on our own terms, and admit or exclude it on the slightest cause. I cannot afford to speak much with my friend. If he is great, he makes me so great that I cannot descend to converse. In the great days, presentiments hover before me, far before me in the firmament. I ought then to dedicate myself to them. I go in that I may seize them, I go out that I may seize them. I fear only that I may lose them receding into the sky in which now they are only a patch of brighter light. Then, though I prize my friends, I cannot afford to talk with them and study their visions, lest I lose my own. It would indeed give me a certain household joy to quit this lofty seeking, this spiritual astronomy, or search of stars, and come down to warm sympathies with you; but then I know well I shall mourn always the vanishing of my mighty gods. It is true, next week I shall have languid times, when I can well afford to occupy myself with foreign objects; then I shall regret the lost literature of your mind, and wish you were by my side again. But if you come, perhaps you will fill my mind only with new visions, not with yourself but with your lustres, and I shall not be able any more than now to converse with you. So I will owe to my friends this evanescent intercourse. I will receive from them not what they have, but what they are. They shall give me that which properly they cannot give me, but which radiates from them. But they shall not hold me by any relations less subtle and pure. We will meet as though we met not, and part as though we parted not.

It has seemed to me lately more possible than I knew, to carry a friendship greatly, on one side, without due correspondence on the other. Why should I cumber myself with the poor fact that the receiver is not capacious? It never troubles the sun that some of his rays fall wide and vain into ungrateful space, and only a small part on the reflecting planet. Let your greatness educate the crude and cold companion. If he is unequal, he will presently pass away, but thou art enlarged by thy own shining; and, no longer a mate for frogs and worms, dost soar and burn with the gods of the empyrean. It is thought a disgrace to love unrequited. But the great will see that true love cannot be unrequited. True love transcends instantly the unworthy object, and dwells and broods on the eternal; and when the poor, interposed mask crumbles, it is not sad, but feels rid of so much earth, and feels its independency the surer. Yet these things may hardly be said without a sort of treachery to the relation. The essence of friendship is entireness, a total magnanimity and trust. It must not surmise or provide for infirmity. It treats its object as a god, that it may deify both.

ALICE EMMA IVES
1876–1930

Born in Detroit, Alice Emma Ives worked as a New York City journalist, poet, drama critic and playwright, penning a total of twenty pieces for the stage. *The Village Postmaster*, a portrayal of mid-nineteenth-century New England life, was a triumph, running to 217 performances. Ives was the first president of the Women's Playwright Society and wrote several feminist plays, including *A Very New Woman*, inspired by the story of Catharine Waugh McCulloch's 1890 partnership in her husband's law firm. Ives' journalism often focused on gender issues: attitudes to suffrage, dress reform and fashion, husbands' control of the domestic purse strings and the like. She achieved some recognition abroad, most notably for *Starr's Girl*, a mining-camp drama which was produced in England before Americans saw it. In the excerpt that follows, Ives addresses the controversial question of whether women can be friends and proves the importance of sisterhood.

'Friendship Among Women',
from *What Can a Woman Do? Or, Her*
Position in the Business and Literary World

Women feel friendship insipid after love, says that dogmatic Frenchman, La Rochefoucauld. And Swift, who ought to have known better, with the example right under his eyes of the life-long affection of Esther Johnson and Lady Gifford, wrote: "To speak the truth, I never yet knew a tolerable woman to be fond of her own sex."

It would scarcely be worth while to attempt to controvert the sweeping assertions of a cynic and a satirist, were it not that even in this advanced age we occasionally hear people of considerable sense advance a like opinion, with every appearance of believing it themselves. Very sad indeed, must be the private experience of any of us who cannot furnish at least one refutation of this charge against womankind.

But if the genuine friendship which exists between women who are unknown to the public, like the testimonials attached to patent medicines, is not likely to be taken as very authentic proof of the value of the article, at least a few instances, of which there is abundant corroboration, in the lives of world-renowned and illustrious women, may serve to prove the truth of our argument.

What devotion could be more lasting and heroic than that of the Princess Lamballe for her unfortunate friend, Marie Antoinette? They had shared each other's confidences in the happy days of prosperity, and, when evil days came upon the queen, the princess could not be persuaded to seek her own safety by leaving the palace. When at last she was summoned to the bedside of a dying relative, Marie Antoinette sent her a letter begging her not to return. "Your heart," she wrote, "would be too deeply wounded; you would have too many tears to shed over my misfortunes, you who love me so tenderly. Adieu, my dear Lamballe; I am always thinking of you, and you know I never change!" But the princess hastened back to her imperiled friend, and all through those terrible last days of the sack, the pillage, and the prison, clung to her with a devotion as tender as it was heroic. When they strove to draw from her at the trial something prejudicial to the royal victim, when the mob which had lost the semblance of humanity, with wild, red eyes, howled like wolves for blood, she preferred death to treachery, and her beautiful head, with its wealth of golden locks, in which was concealed this last letter from Marie Antoinette, was elevated on a pike before the prison window of the woman for whom she had died.

Whatever may have been said derogatory to this

daughter of Maria Theresa, the fact stands proved that a woman who could inspire and hold such a devoted and noble friendship must have had elements of character equally lofty and beautiful.

Scarcely less touching and heroic was the attachment of Catherine Douglas to Lady Joan Beaufort, consort of James I. of Scotland, to whom she was maid of honor. On that terrible night of February 20, 1437, when three hundred assassins, led by the earl of Atholl, "were forcing their way into the royal chamber, Catherine thrust her beautiful arm into the stanchion of the door as a bolt, and held it there till it was broken."

The poet Chaucer had good cause to lament the presence of a powerful lady rival in the affections of his intended bride, who for this reason kept him waiting eight years for her hand. Philippa Picard was the favorite of the queen of Edward the Third, and, being warmly attached to her royal friend, she vowed she would not marry while the latter lived; and so the father of English poetry was forced to possess his soul in patience until the death of the queen set his affianced free.

Mary Stuart's four maids of honor, Mary Fleming, Mary Beton, Mary Livingston, and Mary Seton, "the Queen's Marys," as they were called, with the exception of one who through illness was obliged to retire to a convent, never left their royal mistress while she lived, but supported and comforted her even to the block.

A friendship which provoked the good-natured ridicule of the day was that of Madame Salvage de Faverolles for Hortense, daughter of Joséphine, and queen of Holland. Madame was jocosely called the queen's bodyguard, as she seemed to be her shadow on all occasions. But when in the last illness of Hortense she still remained her shadow, never leaving her day or night, and after her friend's death faithfully carried out the instructions of the will, the jokers were silent.

Hannah More, who wrote the tragedy of Percy for David Garrick, and whose fame as a dramatist was wide in her day, became so attached to Mrs. Garrick after the tragedian's death that the widow fondly called Miss More her chaplain.

Miss Elizabeth Carter, who enjoyed the friendship of Dr. Johnson and other great men of that time, had a devoted confidante in the person of Miss Catherine Talbot. They shared their secrets, and corresponded regularly for thirty years. Never in all that time was there one instance of betrayal or misunderstanding. Think of that, ye croakers and cynics, who are forever saying "a woman can't keep a secret!" Think of keeping hundreds of secrets, and for thirty years, too! If there are any men who can boast of a more extended confidence and friendship, we have never known them.

Anna Seward, admired in her generation as a beauty and a writer, was the devoted friend of the lovely Honora Sneyd, of whom Major André was the rejected lover. "Ah," writes Miss Seward, "how deeply was I a fellow sufferer with Major André, on her marriage! We both lost her forever."

Miss Seward's once famous "Monody on Major André," in which she severely censured Washington for his part in the execution of the unfortunate young officer, was the source of so much grief and mortification to the general that, after peace was concluded between this country and Great Britain, he sent an officer to the English lady, with papers showing how he had labored to save André. "On examining them," she writes to the Ladies of Llangollen, "I found they entirely acquitted the general. They filled me with contrition for the rash injustice of my censure."

The Ladies of Llangollen, above referred to, were perhaps the most romantic and remarkable instances of single-hearted devotion on record. William R. Alger has given a most delightful account of them, from which we condense the following: In the latter part of the eighteenth century Lady Eleanor

Butler and Miss Sarah Ponsonby conceived for each other such a violent affection that they determined to forsake the social world, and pass the remainder of their lives together. Accordingly they departed to an obscure retreat in the country, but their relatives, strongly objecting to such an eccentric proceeding, traced out their hiding-place, and succeeded in separating and bringing them back. Opposition in nowise dampened their ardor, and they determined that their second elopement should be a more successful one. Confiding their secret only to a single faithful servant, they fled. They chose the romantic valley of Llangollen, in Wales, one of the quietest and loveliest spots in the world. Here they bought a tiny cottage, which they fitted with every comfort, and furnished with books, pictures, and all the necessities of two elegant, cultured women. Their neighbors, ignorant of their names, called them "the Ladies of the Vale." "For a quarter of a century, it is said, they never spent twenty-four hours at a time out of their happy valley." They seem never to have wearied of each other, or to have had even the slightest misunderstanding.

A faithful servant, who had been much attached to them, set out several times to search for the young ladies in vain. They, happening to hear of her unsuccessful attempts, sent for the woman, and she lived and died of old age in their service.

After a time the story of this romantic friendship began to be noised abroad, and brought many distinguished visitors to the little cottage in Llangollen. Quite a number of these guests became sincerely attached to their entertainers, and an extensive correspondence was the result. Madame de Genlis wrote enthusiastically of her stay with them. She spoke of the exquisite taste of their tiny establishment, and especially of the Aeolian harp they had in the library window, which she then heard for the first time. Both of the ladies read and spoke most of the modern languages, and Miss Seward, in describing the library of "the two Minervas," speaks of the finest editions, superbly bound, of the best authors of prose and verse in the English, French and Italian languages. They were especially admirers of Dante. Miss Seward paid many tributes in verse to their charming retreat, which she called the "Cambrian Arden," and the two ladies "the Rosalind and Celia of real life."

Miss Martineau visited them in their old age, and describes as something unique these ancient dames in their riding habits, with the rolled and powdered hair, and stately manners of a past century. They declared that they had never, even in the long winters of imprisoning snows, felt a desire to return to the world they had abandoned. Miss Sarah Ponsonby lived to be seventy-six years of age, and Lady Eleanor Charlotte Butler to be ninety. Their deaths were only two years apart. Thus for nearly three score years lived together two of the most devoted friends the world has ever known. Their last resting-place, with that of the faithful servant, can be seen to-day, marked by a marble tombstone, in the old churchyard of the little Welsh village, set in the velvety green of its valley, and shadowed by the rugged hills of Llangollen.

A world-renowned friendship was that of the brilliantly-gifted Madame de Staël and the most celebrated beauty of her time, Madame Récamier. Margaret Fuller, after seeing an engraving of the latter, records in her diary the following: "I have so often thought over the intimacy between her and Madame de Staël. It is so true that a woman may be in love with a woman, and a man with a man." Madame Récamier had an enthusiastic appreciation of the genius of her friend, and Madame de Staël in return felt a sort of intoxication of happiness in the society of the beautiful young creature, whose sincerity, purity and loftiness of character, together with other charming attributes, never failed to attract and fascinate. Sainte-Beuve said that she brought the art of friendship to perfection, and Luyster that she "seemed to possess some talisman by whose spell she disarmed envy and silenced detraction." It need scarcely be hinted that the talisman was innate unselfishness, sweet kindliness and tact. Of the first meeting of these two remarkable women Madame Récamier says: "That day was an epoch in my life."

On the banishment of Madame de Staël, Madame Récamier risked the displeasure of Napoleon in order to visit her friend, for which action she also was banished. During this sad period the two kept up an incessant correspondence. On one occasion, after receiving a present from her "dear Juliette," Madame de Staël writes: "Dear friend, how this dress has touched me! I shall wear it on Tuesday in taking leave of the court. I shall tell everybody that it is a gift from you, and shall make all the men sigh that it is not you who are wearing it."

Again she writes from Blois: "Dear Juliette—Our stay here is drawing to a close. I cannot conceive of either country or home life without you. I know that certain sentiments seem to be more necessary to me; but I also know that everything falls to pieces when you leave." In another letter she says: "Your friendship is like the spring in the desert that never fails; and it is this which makes it impossible not to love you."

That Madame de Staël's estimate of her friend was correct, subsequent events most unmistakably demonstrated. Death only ended this beautiful attachment. The devotion of Madame Récamier to the memory of the illustrious author, and her efforts to disseminate her writings were not less earnest and genuine than had been her affection for her living friend.

The fascination of this delightful subject might make one, like the brook, "go on forever," were it not for a wholesome fear of readers less enthusiastic on this point than the writer. But certainly examples similar to the foregoing might be multiplied to fill volumes. How much might be said of such pairs of friends as Elizabeth Barrett Browning and Mary Mitford, Joanna Baillie and Miss Aiken, Mrs. Hemans and Miss Jewsbury, Madame Swetchine and Romandra Stourdza, Margaret Fuller and the Marchioness Arconati, L. Maria Child and Lucy Osgood, and Sarah Austin and the Duchess of Orleans.

It seems as if each and every one of these said to us: "Dear sister woman, you cannot afford to do without such a necessity as a true, devoted friend. You cannot afford to forego the uplifting of soul, the broadening and sweetening of your life, which such an experience brings. They who are forever sufficient unto themselves must be either gods or fiends; they are not human. The most shrinking, sensitive temperament that shuns all social life has need of one friend, as Michelangelo had of Vittoria Colonna. Do not expect perfection, but cover small faults with the mantle of sweet charity, and don't lift up the corner of the mantle to see if they are still thriving; search, search, search for what is nobler. As elevating and beautiful as are these friendships we have been considering, be sure that one breath of envy, petty spite, narrowness, or uncharitableness would have killed them as dead as an Easter lily under the hot blast of the desert. Do men gather grapes of thorns?"

HARRIET JACOBS
c. 1813–1897

Born into slavery nearly half a century before the Emancipation Proclamation, Jacobs was the first woman in the United States to write her own slave narrative. *Incidents in the Life of a Slave Girl* addressed female slaves' sexual exploitation and told how, by hiding for seven years in an attic space so small she could not stand to her full height, Jacobs was eventually able to escape. Once in the North, she lived as a fugitive slave for a decade, working with abolitionists and finding employment as a nursemaid. In 1852, her Boston employer bought her freedom and Jacobs published her survival story. In the excerpt that follows, Jacobs shares a moving account of her status as a legal outcast in a racist society and the woman whose kindness and conversation restored her trust.

from *Incidents in the Life of a Slave Girl*

CHAPTER XXXIII.

A HOME FOUND

My greatest anxiety now was to obtain employment. My health was greatly improved, though my limbs continued to trouble me with swelling whenever I walked much. The greatest difficulty in my way was, that those who employed strangers required a recommendation; and in my peculiar position, I could, of course, obtain no certificates from the families I had so faithfully served.

One day an acquaintance told me of a lady who wanted a nurse for her babe, and I immediately applied for the situation. The lady told me she preferred to have one who had been a mother, and accustomed to the care of infants. I told her I had nursed two babes of my own. She asked me many questions, but, to my great relief, did not require a recommendation from my former employers. She told me she was an English woman, and that was a pleasant circumstance to me, because I had heard they had less prejudice against color than Americans entertained. It was agreed that we should try each other for a week. The trial proved satisfactory to both parties, and I was engaged for a month.

The heavenly Father had been most merciful to

me in leading me to this place. Mrs. Bruce was a kind and gentle lady, and proved a true and sympathizing friend. Before the stipulated month expired, the necessity of passing up and down stairs frequently, caused my limbs to swell so painfully, that I became unable to perform my duties. Many ladies would have thoughtlessly discharged me; but Mrs. Bruce made arrangements to save me steps, and employed a physician to attend upon me. I had not yet told her that I was a fugitive slave. She noticed that I was often sad, and kindly inquired the cause. I spoke of being separated from my children, and from relatives who were dear to me; but I did not mention the constant feeling of insecurity which oppressed my spirits. I longed for some one to confide in; but I had been so deceived by white people, that I had lost all confidence in them. If they spoke kind words to me, I thought it was for some selfish purpose. I had entered this family with the distrustful feelings I had brought with me out of slavery; but ere six months had passed, I found that the gentle deportment of Mrs. Bruce and the smiles of her lovely babe were thawing my chilled heart. My narrow mind also began to expand under the influences of her intelligent conversation, and the opportunities for reading, which were gladly allowed me whenever I had leisure from my duties. I gradually became more energetic and more cheerful.

The old feeling of insecurity, especially with regard to my children, often threw its dark shadow across my sunshine. Mrs. Bruce offered me a home for Ellen; but pleasant as it would have been, I did not dare to accept it, for fear of offending the Hobbs family. Their knowledge of my precarious situation placed me in their power; and I felt that it was important for me to keep on the right side of them, till, by dint of labor and economy, I could make a home for my children. I was far from feeling satisfied with Ellen's situation. She was not well cared for. She sometimes came to New York to visit me; but she generally brought a request from Mrs. Hobbs that I would buy her a pair of shoes, or some article of clothing. This was accompanied by a promise of payment when Mr. Hobbs's salary at the Custom House became due; but some how or other the pay-day never came. Thus many dollars of my earnings were expended to keep my child comfortably clothed. That, however, was a slight trouble, compared with the fear that their pecuniary embarrassments might induce them to sell my precious young daughter. I knew they were in constant communication with Southerners, and had frequent opportunities to do it. I have stated that when

Dr. Flint put Ellen in jail, at two years old, she had an inflammation of the eyes, occasioned by measles. This disease still troubled her; and kind Mrs. Bruce proposed that she should come to New York for a while, to be under the care of Dr. Elliott, a well known oculist. It did not occur to me that there was any thing improper in a mother's making such a request; but Mrs. Hobbs was very angry, and refused to let her go. Situated as I was, it was not politic to insist upon it. I made no complaint, but I longed to be entirely free to act a mother's part towards my children. The next time I went over to Brooklyn, Mrs. Hobbs, as if to apologize for her anger, told me she had employed her own physician to attend to Ellen's eyes, and that she had refused my request because she did not consider it safe to trust her in New York. I accepted the explanation in silence; but she had told me that my child *belonged* to her daughter, and I suspected that her real motive was a fear of my conveying her property away from her. Perhaps I did her injustice; but my knowledge of Southerners made it difficult for me to feel otherwise.

Sweet and bitter were mixed in the cup of my life, and I was thankful that it had ceased to be entirely bitter. I loved Mrs. Bruce's babe. When it laughed and crowed in my face, and twined its little tender arms confidingly about my neck, it made me think of the time when Benny and Ellen were babies, and my wounded heart was soothed. One bright morning, as I stood at the window, tossing baby in my arms, my attention was attracted by a young man in sailor's dress, who was closely observing every house as he passed. I looked at him earnestly. Could it be my brother William? It *must* be he—and yet, how changed! I placed the baby safely, flew down stairs, opened the front door, beckoned to the sailor, and in less than a minute I was clasped in my brother's arms. How much we had to tell each other! How we laughed, and how we cried, over each other's adventures! I took him to Brooklyn, and again saw him with Ellen, the dear child whom he had loved and tended so carefully, while I was shut up in my miserable den. He staid in New York a week. His old feelings of affection for me and Ellen were as lively as ever. There are no bonds so strong as those which are formed by suffering together.

SARAH ORNE JEWETT
1849–1909

One of the pioneers of American regionalism, Jewett's unique attention to local scenes of domestic life enabled her to capture its thick silences and everyday intimacies. The novelist Henry James admired 'her beautiful little quantum of achievement.' *The Country of the Pointed Firs* tells the story of a visitor to a small, close-knit Maine community. Using a regional sensibility similar to Elizabeth Gaskell's *Cranford*, Jewett expertly portrays subtle rituals of kinship and hospitality. The novel's central chapter, excerpted here, exposes the animosities and sister-like friendships that become apparent at a family reunion. The warm bustle of a shared meal amid boisterous children enlivens even the most isolated individuals. Like newly released captives, they flourish in good company. Though introverts may not crave sociable occasions, it's clear that ties to nature and community do nurture them socially and spiritually. After all, no man is an island unto himself.

from *The Country of the Pointed Firs*

CHAPTER XVIII.

THE BOWDEN REUNION

It is very rare in country life, where high days and holidays are few, that any occasion of general interest proves to be less than great. Such is the hidden fire of enthusiasm in the New England nature that, once given an outlet, it shines forth with almost volcanic light and heat. In quiet neighborhoods such inward force does not waste itself upon those petty excitements of every day that belong to cities, but when, at long intervals, the altars to patriotism, to friendship, to the ties of kindred, are reared in our familiar fields, then the fires glow, the flames come up as if from the inexhaustible burning heart of the earth; the primal fires break through the granite dust in which our souls are set. Each heart is warm and every face shines with the ancient light. Such a day as this has transfiguring powers, and easily makes friends of those who have been cold-hearted, and gives to those who are dumb their chance to speak, and lends some beauty to the plainest face.

"Oh, I expect I shall meet friends today that I haven't seen in a long while," said Mrs. Blackett with deep satisfaction. "'T will bring out a good many of the old folks, 't is such a lovely day. I'm always glad not to have them disappointed."

"I guess likely the best of 'em 'll be there," answered Mrs. Todd with gentle humor, stealing a glance at me. "There's one thing certain: there's nothing takes in this whole neighborhood like anything related to the Bowdens. Yes, I do feel that when you call upon the Bowdens you may expect most families to rise up between the Landing and the far end of the Back Cove. Those that aren't kin by blood are kin by marriage."

"There used to be an old story goin' about when I was a girl," said Mrs. Blackett, with much amusement. "There was a great many more Bowdens then than there are now, and the folks was all setting in meeting a dreadful hot Sunday afternoon, and a scatter-witted little bound girl came running to the meetin'-house door all out o' breath from somewheres in the neighborhood. 'Mis' Bowden, Mis' Bowden!' says she. 'Your baby's in a fit!' They used to tell that the whole congregation was up on its feet in a minute and right out into the aisles. All the Mis' Bowdens was setting right out for home; the minister stood there in the pulpit tryin' to keep sober, an' all at once he burst right out laughin'. He was a very nice man, they said, and he said he'd better give 'em the benediction, and they could hear the sermon next Sunday, so he kept it over. My mother was here, and she thought certain 't was me."

"None of our family was ever subject to fits," interrupted Mrs. Todd severely. "No, we never had fits, none of us, and 't was lucky we didn't 'way out here to Green Island. Now these folks right in front: dear sakes knows the bunches o' soothing catnip an' yarrow I've had to favor old Mis' Evins with dryin'! You can see it right in their expressions, all them Evins folks. There, just you look up to the cross-roads, mother," she suddenly exclaimed. "See all the teams ahead of us. And oh, look down on the bay; yes, look down on the bay! See what a sight o' boats, all headin' for the Bowden place cove!"

"Oh, ain't it beautiful!" said Mrs. Blackett, with all the delight of a girl. She stood up in the high wagon to see everything, and when she sat down again she took fast hold of my hand.

"Hadn't you better urge the horse a little, Almiry?" she asked. "He's had it easy as we came along, and he can rest when we get there. The others are some little ways ahead, and I don't want to lose a minute."

We watched the boats drop their sails one by one in the cove as we drove along the high land. The old Bowden house stood, low-storied and broad-roofed, in its green fields as if it were a motherly brown hen

113

waiting for the flock that came straying toward it from every direction. The first Bowden settler had made his home there, and it was still the Bowden farm; five generations of sailors and farmers and soldiers had been its children. And presently Mrs. Blackett showed me the stone-walled burying-ground that stood like a little fort on a knoll overlooking the bay, but, as she said, there were plenty of scattered Bowdens who were not laid there—some lost at sea, and some out West, and some who died in the war; most of the home graves were those of women.

We could see now that there were different foot-paths from along shore and across country. In all these there were straggling processions walking in single file, like old illustrations of the Pilgrim's Progress. There was a crowd about the house as if huge bees were swarming in the lilac bushes. Beyond the fields and cove a higher point of land ran out into the bay, covered with woods which must have kept away much of the northwest wind in winter. Now there was a pleasant look of shade and shelter there for the great family meeting.

We hurried on our way, beginning to feel as if we were very late, and it was a great satisfaction at last to turn out of the stony highroad into a green lane shaded with old apple-trees. Mrs. Todd encouraged the horse until he fairly pranced with gayety as we drove round to the front of the house on the soft turf. There was an instant cry of rejoicing, and two or three persons ran toward us from the busy group.

"Why, dear Mis' Blackett!—here's Mis' Blackett!" I heard them say, as if it were pleasure enough for one day to have a sight of her. Mrs. Todd turned to me with a lovely look of triumph and self-forgetfulness. An elderly man who wore the look of a prosperous sea-captain put up both arms and lifted Mrs. Blackett down from the high wagon like a child, and kissed her with hearty affection. "I was master afraid she wouldn't be here," he said, looking at Mrs. Todd with a face like a happy sunburnt schoolboy, while everybody crowded round to give their welcome.

"Mother's always the queen," said Mrs. Todd. "Yes, they'll all make everything of mother; she'll have a lovely time to-day. I wouldn't have had her miss it, and there won't be a thing she'll ever regret, except to mourn because William wa'n't here."

Mrs. Blackett having been properly escorted to the house, Mrs. Todd received her own full share of honor, and some of the men, with a simple kindness that was the soul of chivalry, waited upon us and our baskets and led away the white horse. I already knew some of Mrs. Todd's friends and kindred, and felt like an adopted Bowden in this happy moment. It seemed to be enough for any one to have arrived by the same conveyance as Mrs. Blackett, who presently had her court inside the house, while Mrs. Todd, large, hospitable, and preeminent, was the centre of a rapidly increasing crowd about the lilac bushes. Small companies were continually coming up the long green slope from the water, and nearly all the boats had come to shore. I counted three or four that were baffled by the light breeze, but before long all the Bowdens, small and great, seemed to have assembled, and we started to go up to the grove across the field.

Out of the chattering crowd of noisy children, and large-waisted women whose best black dresses fell straight to the ground in generous folds, and sunburnt men who looked as serious as if it were town-meeting day, there suddenly came silence and order. I saw the straight, soldierly little figure of a man who bore a fine resemblance to Mrs. Blackett, and who appeared to marshal us with perfect ease. He was imperative enough, but with a grand military sort of courtesy, and bore himself with solemn dignity of importance. We were sorted out according to some clear design of his own, and stood as speechless as a troop to await his orders. Even the children were ready to march together, a pretty flock, and at

the last moment Mrs. Blackett and a few distinguished companions, the ministers and those who
were very old, came out of the house together and
took their places. We ranked by fours, and even then
we made a long procession.

There was a wide path mowed for us across the
field, and, as we moved along, the birds flew up out
of the thick second crop of clover, and the bees
hummed as if it still were June. There was a flashing
of white gulls over the water where the fleet of boats
rode the low waves together in the cove, swaying
their small masts as if they kept time to our steps.
The plash of the water could be heard faintly, yet
still be heard; we might have been a company of
ancient Greeks going to celebrate a victory, or to
worship the god of harvests in the grove above. It
was strangely moving to see this and to make part of
it. The sky, the sea, have watched poor humanity at
its rites so long; we were no more a New England
family celebrating its own existence and simple progress; we carried the tokens and inheritance of all
such households from which this had descended,
and were only the latest of our line. We possessed the
instincts of a far, forgotten childhood; I found
myself thinking that we ought to be carrying green
branches and singing as we went. So we came to the
thick shaded grove still silent, and were set in our

places by the straight trees that swayed together and let sunshine through here and there like a single golden leaf that flickered down, vanishing in the cool shade.

The grove was so large that the great family looked far smaller than it had in the open field; there was a thick growth of dark pines and firs with an occasional maple or oak that gave a gleam of color like a bright window in the great roof. On three sides we could see the water, shining behind the tree-trunks, and feel the cool salt breeze that began to come up with the tide just as the day reached its highest point of heat. We could see the green sunlit field we had just crossed as if we looked out at it from a dark room, and the old house and its lilacs standing placidly in the sun, and the great barn with a stockade of carriages from which two or three care-taking men who had lingered were coming across the field together. Mrs. Todd had taken off her warm gloves and looked the picture of content.

"There!" she exclaimed. "I've always meant to have you see this place, but I never looked for such a beautiful opportunity—weather an' occasion both made to match. Yes, it suits me: I don't ask no more I want to know if you saw mother walkin' at the head! It choked me right up to see mother at the head, walkin' with the ministers," and Mrs. Todd turned away to hide the feelings she could not instantly control.

"Who was the marshal?" I hastened to ask. "Was he an old soldier?"

"Don't he do well?" answered Mrs. Todd with satisfaction.

"He don't often have such a chance to show off his gifts," said Mrs. Caplin, a friend from the Landing who had joined us. "That's Sant Bowden; he always takes the lead, such days. Good for nothing else most o' his time; trouble is, he"—

I turned with interest to hear the worst. Mrs. Caplin's tone was both zealous and impressive.

"Stim'lates," she explained scornfully.

"No, Santin never was in the war," said Mrs. Todd with lofty indifference. "It was a cause of real distress to him. He kep' enlistin', and traveled far an' wide about here, an' even took the bo't and went to Boston to volunteer; but he ain't a sound man, an' they wouldn't have him. They say he knows all their tactics, an' can tell all about the battle o' Waterloo well 's he can Bunker Hill. I told him once the country'd lost a great general, an' I meant it, too."

"I expect you're near right," said Mrs. Caplin, a little crestfallen and apologetic.

"I be right," insisted Mrs. Todd with much amiability. "'T was most too bad to cramp him down to his peaceful trade, but he's a most excellent shoemaker at his best, an' he always says it's a trade that gives him time to think an' plan his manœuvres. Over to the Port they always invite him to march Decoration Day, same as the rest, an' he does look noble; he comes of soldier stock."

I had been noticing with great interest the curiously French type of face which prevailed in this rustic company. I had said to myself before that Mrs. Blackett was plainly of French descent, in both her appearance and her charming gifts, but this is not surprising when one has learned how large a proportion of the early settlers on this northern coast of New England were of Huguenot blood, and that it is the Norman Englishman, not the Saxon, who goes adventuring to a new world.

"They used to say in old times," said Mrs. Todd modestly, "that our family came of very high folks in France, and one of 'em was a great general in some o' the old wars. I sometimes think that Santin's ability has come 'way down from then. 'T ain't nothin' he's ever acquired; 't was born in him. I don't know 's he ever saw a fine parade, or met with those that studied up such things. He's figured it all out an' got his papers so he knows how to aim a cannon right for William's fish-house five miles out on Green Island, or up there on Burnt Island where the signal is. He had it all over to me one day, an' I tried hard to appear interested. His life's all in it, but he will have those poor gloomy spells come over him now an' then, an' then he has to drink."

Mrs. Caplin gave a heavy sigh.

"There's a great many such strayaway folks, just as there is plants," continued Mrs. Todd, who was nothing if not botanical. "I know of just one sprig of laurel that grows over back here in a wild spot, an' I never could hear of no other on this coast. I had a large bunch brought me once from Massachusetts way, so I know it. This piece grows in an open spot where you'd think 't would do well, but it's sort o' poor-lookin'. I've visited it time an' again, just to notice its poor blooms. 'T is a real Sant Bowden, out of its own place."

Mrs. Caplin looked bewildered and blank. "Well, all I know is, last year he worked out some kind of a plan so 's to parade the county conference in pla-toons, and got 'em all flustered up tryin' to sense his ideas of a holler square," she burst forth. "They was holler enough anyway after ridin' 'way down from up country into the salt air, and they'd been treated to a sermon on faith an' works from old Fayther Harlow that never knows when to cease. 'T wa'n't no time for tactics then—they wa'n't a-thinkin' of the church military. Sant, he couldn't do nothin' with 'em. All he thinks of, when he sees a crowd, is how to march 'em. 'T is all very well when he don't 'tempt too much. He never did act like other folks."

"Ain't I just been maintainin' that he ain't like 'em?" urged Mrs. Todd decidedly. "Strange folks has got to have strange ways, for what I see."

"Somebody observed once that you could pick out the likeness of 'most every sort of a foreigner when you looked about you in our parish," said Sister Caplin, her face brightening with sudden illumination. "I didn't see the bearin' of it then quite so plain. I always did think Mari' Harris resembled a Chinee."

"Mari' Harris was pretty as a child, I remember," said the pleasant voice of Mrs. Blackett, who, after receiving the affectionate greetings of nearly the whole company, came to join us—to see, as she insisted, that we were out of mischief.

"Yes, Mari' was one o' them pretty little lambs that make dreadful homely old sheep," replied Mrs. Todd with energy. "Cap'n Littlepage never 'd look so disconsolate if she was any sort of a proper person to direct things. She might divert him; yes, she might divert the old gentleman, an' let him think he had his own way, 'stead o' arguing everything down to the bare bone. 'T wouldn't hurt her to sit down an' hear his great stories once in a while."

"The stories are very interesting," I ventured to say.

"Yes, you always catch yourself a-thinkin' what if they was all true, and he had the right of it," answered Mrs. Todd. "He's a good sight better company, though dreamy, than such sordid creatur's as Mari' Harris."

"Live and let live," said dear old Mrs. Blackett gently. "I haven't seen the captain for a good while, now that I ain't so constant to meetin'," she added wistfully. "We always have known each other."

"Why, if it is a good pleasant day tomorrow, I'll get William to call an' invite the capt'in to dinner. William'll be in early so 's to pass up the street without meetin' anybody."

"There, they're callin' out it's time to set the tables," said Mrs. Caplin, with great excitement.

"Here's Cousin Sarah Jane Blackett! Well, I am pleased, certain!" exclaimed Mrs. Todd, with unaffected delight; and these kindred spirits met and parted with the promise of a good talk later on. After this there was no more time for conversation until we were seated in order at the long tables.

"I'm one that always dreads seeing some o' the folks that I don't like, at such a time as this," announced Mrs. Todd privately to me after a season of reflection. We were just waiting for the feast to begin. "You wouldn't think such a great creatur' 's I be could feel all over pins an' needles. I remember, the day I promised to Nathan, how it come over me, just 's I was feelin' happy 's I could, that I'd got to have an own cousin o' his for my near relation all the rest o' my life, an' it seemed as if die I should. Poor Nathan saw somethin' had crossed me—he had very nice feelings—and when he asked me what 't was, I told him. 'I never could like her myself,' said he. 'You sha'n't be bothered, dear,' he says; an' 't was one o' the things that made me set a good deal by Nathan, he didn't make a habit of always opposin', like some men. 'Yes,' says I, 'but think o' Thanksgivin' times an' funerals; she's our relation, an' we've got to own her.' Young folks don't think o' those things. There she goes now, do let's pray her by!" said Mrs. Todd, with an alarming transition from general opinions to particular animosities. "I hate her just the same as I always did; but she's got on a real pretty dress. I do try to remember that she's Nathan's cousin. Oh dear, well; she's gone by after all, an' ain't seen me. I expected she'd come pleasantin' round just to show off an' say afterwards she was acquainted."

This was so different from Mrs. Todd's usual largeness of mind that I had a moment's uneasiness;

but the cloud passed quickly over her spirit, and was gone with the offender.

There never was a more generous out-of-door feast along the coast than the Bowden family set forth that day. To call it a picnic would make it seem trivial. The great tables were edged with pretty oak-leaf trimming, which the boys and girls made. We brought flowers from the fence-thickets of the great field; and out of the disorder of flowers and provisions suddenly appeared as orderly a scheme for the feast as the marshal had shaped for the procession. I began to respect the Bowdens for their inheritance of good taste and skill and a certain pleasing gift of formality. Something made them do all these things in a finer way than most country people would have done them. As I looked up and down the tables there was a good cheer, a grave soberness that shone with pleasure, a humble dignity of bearing. There were some who should have sat below the salt for lack of this good breeding; but they were not many. So, I said to myself, their ancestors may have sat in the great hall of some old French house in the Middle Ages, when battles and sieges and processions and feasts were familiar things. The ministers and Mrs. Blackett, with a few of their rank and age, were put in places of honor, and for once that

I looked any other way I looked twice at Mrs. Blackett's face, serene and mindful of privilege and responsibility, the mistress by simple fitness of this great day.

Mrs. Todd looked up at the roof of green trees, and then carefully surveyed the company. "I see 'em better now they're all settin' down," she said with satisfaction. "There's old Mr. Gilbraith and his sister. I wish they were settin' with us; they're not among folks they can parley with, an' they look disappointed."

As the feast went on, the spirits of my companion steadily rose. The excitement of an unexpectedly great occasion was a subtle stimulant to her disposition, and I could see that sometimes when Mrs. Todd had seemed limited and heavily domestic, she had simply grown sluggish for lack of proper surroundings. She was not so much reminiscent now as expectant, and as alert and gay as a girl. We who were her neighbors were full of gayety, which was but the reflected light from her beaming countenance. It was not the first time that I was full of wonder at the waste of human ability in this world, as a botanist wonders at the wastefulness of nature, the thousand seeds that die, the unused provision of every sort. The reserve force of society grows more and more amazing to one's thought. More than one

face among the Bowdens showed that only opportunity and stimulus were lacking—a narrow set of
circumstances had caged a fine able character and
held it captive. One sees exactly the same types in a
country gathering as in the most brilliant city company. You are safe to be understood if the spirit of
your speech is the same for one neighbor as for
the other.

❧

SAMUEL JOHNSON
1709–1784

Johnson's prolific writings encompass many styles: journalism (he founded the *Rambler*), poetry, drama, biography (*The Lives of the English Poets*), romance (*The History of Rasselas, Prince of Abissinia*), records (*Parliamentary Debates*, his compendium of contemporary political speeches). His acumen and poetic precision have been praised by generations of critics, and T. S. Eliot admired 'the certainty, the ease with which he hits the bull's-eye every time.' Johnson's dictionary, begun in 1747 and published in 1755, fixed pronunciations and defined upwards of 40,000 words, enduring as an unparalleled resource until *The Oxford English Dictionary*'s publication, two centuries later. His friend Thomas Davies's Covent Garden bookshop was the setting for his pivotal first encounter with the Scot James Boswell, who was to become his biographer, thus immortalizing in his diaries the everyday talk and idiosyncrasies that enlivened Johnson's literary eminence. In the excerpt that follows, Johnson reflects on the causes of friendship's demise, observing that true friends are rare and that conflicts of interest, suspicions and anger can be overcome if the relationship is not allowed to deteriorate so badly that the desire to please each other vanishes.

'The Decay of Friendship',
from *The Idler*, Saturday Sept. 23, 1758

Life has no pleasure higher or nobler than that of friendship. It is painful to consider, that this sublime enjoyment may be impaired or destroyed by innumerable causes, and that there is no human possession of which the duration is less certain.

Many have talked, in very exalted language, of the perpetuity of friendship, of invincible constancy, and unalienable kindness; and some examples have been seen of men who have continued faithful to their earliest choice, and whose affection has predominated over changes of fortune, and contrariety of opinion.

But these instances are memorable, because they are rare. The friendship which is to be practised or expected by common mortals, must take its rise from mutual pleasure, and must end when power ceases of delighting each other.

Many accidents therefore may happen, by which the ardour of kindness will be abated, without criminal baseness or contemptible inconstancy on either part. To give pleasure is not always in our power; and little does he know himself, who believes that he can be always able to receive it.

Those who would gladly pass their days together

may be separated by the different course of their affairs; and friendship, like love, is destroyed by long absence, though it may be increased by short intermissions. What we have missed long enough to want it, we value more when it is regained; but that which has been lost till it is forgotten, will be found at last with little gladness, and with still less, if a substitute has supplied the place. A man deprived of the companion to whom he used to open his bosom, and with whom he shared the hours of leisure and merriment, feels the day at first hanging heavy on him; his difficulties oppress, and his doubts distract him; he sees time come and go without his wonted gratification, and all is sadness within and solitude about him. But this uneasiness never lasts long; necessity produces expedients, new amusements are discovered, and new conversation is admitted.

No expectation is more frequently disappointed, than that which naturally arises in the mind from the prospect of meeting an old friend after long separation. We expect the attraction to be revived, and the coalition to be renewed; no man considers how much alteration time has made in himself, and very few inquire what effect it has had upon others. The first hour convinces them, that the pleasure which they have formerly enjoyed, is forever at an end; different scenes have made different impressions; the opinions of both are changed; and that similitude of manners and sentiment is lost which confirmed them both in the approbation of themselves.

Friendship is often destroyed by opposition of interest, not only by the ponderous and visible interest which the desire of wealth and greatness forms and maintains, but by a thousand secret and slight competitions, scarcely known to the mind upon which they operate. There is scarcely any man without some favourite trifle which he values above greater attainments, some desire of petty praise which he cannot patiently suffer to be frustrated. This minute ambition is sometimes crossed before it is known, and sometimes defeated by wanton petulance; but such attacks are seldom made without the loss of friendship; for whoever has once found the vulnerable part will always be feared, and the resentment will burn on in secret, of which shame hinders the discovery.

This, however, is a slow malignity, which a wise man will obviate as inconsistent with quiet, and a good man will repress as contrary to virtue; but human happiness is sometimes violated by some more sudden strokes.

A dispute begun in jest upon a subject which a moment before was on both parts regarded with careless indifference, is continued by the desire of conquest, till vanity kindles into rage, and opposition rankles into enmity. Against this hasty mischief, I know not what security can be obtained; men will be sometimes surprised into quarrels; and though they might both hasten to reconciliation, as soon as their tumult had subsided, yet two minds will seldom be found together, which can at once subdue their discontent, or immediately enjoy the sweets of peace, without remembering the wounds of the conflict.

Friendship has other enemies. Suspicion is always hardening the cautious, and disgust repelling the delicate. Very slender differences will sometimes part those whom long reciprocation of civility or beneficence has united. Lonelove and Ranger retired into the country to enjoy the company of each other, and returned in six weeks cold and petulant: Ranger's pleasure was, to walk in the fields, and Lonelove's to sit in a bower; each had complied with the other in his turn, and each was angry that compliance had been exacted.

The most fatal disease of friendship is gradual decay, or dislike hourly increased by causes too slender for complaint and too numerous for removal. Those who are angry may be reconciled; those who have been injured may receive a recompense; but when the desire of pleasing and willingness to be pleased is silently diminished, the renovation of friendship is hopeless; as, when the vital powers sink into langour, there is no longer any use of the physician.

AUDRE LORDE
1934–1992

In the 1960s, Lorde became the voice of women and outsiders who had not truly been heard, let alone listened to by mainstream culture. Speak up, she told them, because 'your silence will not protect you.' Celebrated for her feminist theory, pan-Africanism, speeches and poetry, Lorde boldly addressed political, racial and sexual taboos. Her writing drew attention to poor, black, and third-world women, telling their stories and demanding more than tolerance. By nurturing each other, building interracial friendships, and what she termed 'meeting across our differences', she believed they would discover their collective power. Community would lead to self-actualization and liberation. *Zami: A New Spelling of My Name*, whose title derives from the Carribean-French word for lesbians, 'les amies', is a landmark biomythography about a West Indian girl's coming of age. In the excerpt featured here, the narrator describes her joy at discovering sister outsiders.

from *Zami: A New Spelling of My Name*

In high school, my best friends were "The Branded," as our sisterhood of rebels sometimes called ourselves. We never talked about those differences that separated us, only the ones that united us against the *others*. My friends and I talked about who studied German or French, who liked poetry or doing "the twist," who went out with boys, and who was "progressive." We even talked about our position as women in a world supposed to be run by men.

But we never ever talked about what it meant and felt like to be Black and white, and the effects that had on our being friends. Of course, everybody with any sense deplored racial discrimination, theoretically and without discussion. We could conquer it by ignoring it.

I had grown up in such an isolated world that it was hard for me to recognize difference as anything other than a threat, because it usually was. (The first time I saw my sister Helen in the tub naked I was almost fourteen, and I thought she was a witch because her nipples were pale pink against her light brown breasts, not deeply purple like mine.) But sometimes, I was close to crazy with believing that there was some secret thing wrong with me personally that formed an invisible barrier between me and the rest of my friends, who were white. What was it that kept people from inviting me to their houses, their parties, their summer homes for a weekend? Was it that their mothers did not like them to have friends, the way my mother didn't? Did their mothers caution them about never trusting outsiders? But they visited each other. There was something here that I was missing. Since the only place I couldn't see clearly was behind my own eyes, obviously the trouble was with me. I had no words for racism.

We were The Branded, the Lunatic Fringe, proud of our outrageousness and our madness, our bizarre-colored inks and quill pens. We learned how to mock the straight set, and how to cultivate our group paranoia into an instinct for self-protecting that always stopped our shenanigans just short of expulsion. We wrote obscure poetry and cherished our strangeness as the spoils of default, and in the process we learned that pain and rejection hurt, but that they weren't fatal, and that they could be useful since they couldn't be avoided. We learned that not feeling at all was worse than hurting. At that time, suffering was clearly what we did best. We became The Branded because we learned how to make a virtue out of it.

How meager the sustenance was I gained from the four years I spent in high school; yet how important that sustenance was to my survival. Remembering that time is like watching old pictures of myself in a prison camp picking edible scraps out of the garbage heap, and knowing that without that garbage I might have starved to death. The overwhelming racism of so many of the faculty, including the ones upon whom I had my worst schoolgirl crushes. How little I settled for in the way of human contact, compared to what I was conscious of wanting.

It was in high school that I came to believe that I was different from my white classmates, not because I was Black, but because I was me.

For four years, Hunter High School was a lifeline. No matter what it was in reality, I got something there I needed. For the first time I met young women my own age, Black and white, who spoke a language I could usually understand and reply within. I met girls with whom I could share feelings and dreams and ideas without fear. I found adults who tolerated my feelings and ideas without punishment for insolence, and even a few who respected and admired them.

Writing poetry became an ordinary effort, not a secret and rebellious vice. The other girls at Hunter who wrote poetry did not invite me to their homes, either, but they did elect me literary editor of the school arts magazine.

❦

MICHEL DE MONTAIGNE
1533–1592

Montaigne was a French nobleman, legal counsellor, and Renaissance mayor of Bordeaux, but his fame rests on having more or less invented the modern essay. As the French word *essai*, which means 'trial', suggests, this was a form designed to put ideas and opinions up for discussion. This was an approach entirely befitting of a sceptic who inscribed his personal medal with *What do I know?* on one side, and *Restraint* on the other. Etienne de la Boétie, the object of Montaigne's essay on friendship which appears in this volume, was an older judge with whom he shared a bond surpassing the love of women. The pair's uncommon intimacy was based on honest communication, compatibility, trust and moral virtue. Although Montaigne's idealization of de la Boétie is indebted to Renaissance and classical literary conventions, it has often felt like a familiar code to queer readers. Oscar Wilde cited this friendship as an example of 'the love that dare not speak its name' during his 1895 trial for gross indecency.

'Of Friendship'

Having considered the proceedings of a painter that serves me, I had a mind to imitate his way. He chooses the fairest place and middle of any wall, or panel, wherein to draw a picture, which he finishes with his utmost care and art, and the vacuity about it he fills with grotesques, which are odd fantastic figures without any grace but what they derive from their variety, and the extravagance of their shapes. And in truth, what are these things I scribble, other than grotesques and monstrous bodies, made of various parts, without any certain figure, or any other than accidental order, coherence, or proportion?

In this second part I go hand in hand with my painter; but fall very short of him in the first and the better, my power of handling not being such, that I dare to offer at a rich piece, finely polished, and set off according to art. I have therefore thought fit to borrow one of Estienne de la Boetie, and such a one as shall honor and adorn all the rest of my work—namely, a discourse that he called Voluntary Servitude; but, since, those who did not know him have properly enough called it "Le contre Un." He wrote in his youth by way of essay, in honor of liberty against tyrants; and it has since run through the hands of men of great learning and judgment, not without singular and merited commendation; for it is finely written, and as full as anything can possibly be.

And yet one may confidently say it is far short of what he was able to do; and if in that more mature age, wherein I had the happiness to know him, he had taken a design like this of mine, to commit his thoughts to writing, we should have seen a great many rare things, and such as would have gone very near to have rivalled the best writings of antiquity: for in natural parts especially, I know no man comparable to him. But he has left nothing behind him, save this treatise only (and that, too, by chance, for I believe he never saw it after it first went out of his hands), and some observations upon that edict of January, made famous by our civil wars, which also shall elsewhere, peradventure, find a place. These were all I could recover of his remains, I to whom, with so affectionate a remembrance, upon his deathbed, he by his last will bequeathed his library and papers, the little book of his works only excepted, which I committed to the press. And this particular obligation I have to this treatise of his, that it was the occasion of my first coming acquainted with him; for it was showed to me long before I had the good fortune to know him; and gave me the first knowledge of his name, proving the first cause and foundation of a friendship which we afterward improved and maintained, so long as God was pleased to continue us together, so perfect, inviolate, and entire, that certainly the like is hardly to be found in story, and among the men of this age there is no sign nor trace of any such thing in use; so much concurrence is required to the building of such a one, that 'tis much, if fortune bring it but once to pass in three ages.

There is nothing to which nature seems so much to have inclined us as to society; and Aristotle says, that the good legislators had more respect to friendship than to justice. Now the most supreme point of its perfection is this: for, generally, all those that pleasure, profit, public or private interest create and nourish, are so much the less beautiful and generous, and so much the less friendships, by how much they mix another cause, and design, and fruit in friendship, than itself. Neither do the four ancient kinds, natural, social, hospitable, venerian, either separately or jointly, make up a true and perfect friendship.

That of children to parents is rather respect: friendship is nourished by communication, which cannot, by reason of the great disparity, be betwixt these, but would rather perhaps offend the duties of nature; for neither are all the secret thoughts of fathers fit to be communicated to children, lest it beget an indecent familiarity between them; nor can the advices and reproofs, which is one of the principal offices of friendship, be properly performed by the son to the father. There are some countries where 'twas the custom for children to kill their fathers; and others, where the fathers killed their children, to avoid their being an impediment one to another in life; and naturally the expectations of the one depend upon the ruin of the other.

This name of brother does indeed carry with it a fine and delectable sound, and for that reason, he and I called one another brothers, but the complication of interests, the division of estates, and that the wealth of the one should be the poverty of the other, strangely relax and weaken the fraternal tie: brothers pursuing their fortune and advancement by the same path, 'tis hardly possible but they must of necessity often jostle and hinder one another. Besides, why is it necessary that the correspondence of manners, parts, and inclinations, which begets the true and perfect friendships, should always meet in these relations? The father and the son may be of quite contrary humors, and so of brothers: he is my son, he is my brother; but he is passionate, ill-natured, or a fool. And moreover, by how much these are friendships that the law and natural obligation impose upon us, so much less is there of our own choice and voluntary freedom; whereas that voluntary liberty of ours has no production more promptly and properly its own than affection and friendship. Not that I have not in my own person experimented all that can possibly be expected of that kind, having had the best and most indulgent father, even to his extreme old age, that ever was, and who was himself descended from a family for many generations famous and exemplary for brotherly concord.

We are not here to bring the love we bear to women, though it be an act of our own choice, into comparison; nor rank it with the others. "Nor is the goddess unknown to me, who mixes a pleasing sorrow with my love's flame" [Catullus]. The fire of this, I confess, is more active, more eager, and more sharp; but withal, 'tis more precipitant, fickle, moving, and inconstant; a fever subject to intermissions and paroxysms, that has seized but on one part of us. Whereas in friendship, 'tis a general and universal fire, but temperate and equal, a constant established heat, all gentle and smooth, without poignancy or roughness. Moreover, in love, 'tis no other than frantic desire for that which flies from us: "As the hunter pursues the hare, through cold and heat, over hill and dale, but, so soon as it is taken, no longer cares for it, and only delights in chasing that which flees from him" [Ariosto], so soon as it enters into the terms of friendship, that is to say, into a concurrence of desires, it vanishes and is gone, fruition destroys it, as having only a fleshly end, and such a one as is subject to satiety. Friendship, on the contrary, is enjoyed proportionably as it is desired; and only grows up, is nourished and improves by enjoyment, as being of itself spiritual, and the soul growing still more refined by practice. Under this perfect friendship, the other fleeting affections have in my younger years found some place in me, to say nothing of him, who himself so confesses but too much in his verses; so that I had both these passions, but always so, that I could myself well enough distinguish them, and never in any degree of comparison with one another; the first maintaining its flight in so lofty and so brave a place, as with disdain to look down, and see the other flying at a far humbler pitch below.

As concerning marriage, besides that it is a covenant, the entrance into which only is free, but the continuance in it forced and compulsory, having another dependence than that of our own freewill, and a bargain commonly contracted to other ends, there almost always happens a thousand intricacies in it to unravel, enough to break the thread and to divert the current of a lively affection: whereas friendship has no manner of business or traffic with aught but itself. Moreover, to say truth, the ordinary talent of women is not such as is sufficient to maintain the conference and communication required to the support of this scared tie; nor do they appear to be endued with constancy of mind, to sustain the pinch of so hard and durable a knot. And doubtless, if without this, there could be such a free and voluntary familiarity contracted where not only the souls might have this entire fruition, but the bodies also might share in the alliance, and a man be engaged throughout, the friendship would certainly be more full and perfect; but it is without example that this sex has ever yet arrived at such perfection; and by the common consent of the ancient schools, it is wholly rejected from it.

I return to my own more just and true description. "Those are only to be reputed friendships, that are fortified and confirmed by judgment and length of time" [Cicero]. For the rest, what we commonly call friends and friendships, are nothing but acquaintance and familiarities, either occasionally contracted or upon some design, by means of which there happens some little intercourse between our souls. But in the friendship I speak of, they mix and work themselves into one piece, with so universal a mixture, that there is no more sign of the seam by which they were first conjoined. If a man should importune me to give a reason why I loved him, I find it could no otherwise be expressed, than by making answer: because it was he, because it was I. There is, beyond all that I am able to say, I know not what inexplicable and fated power that brought on this union. We sought one another long before we met, and by the characters we heard of one another, which wrought upon our affections more than, in reason, mere reports should do; I think 'twas by some secret appointment of heaven. We embraced in our names; and at our first meeting, which was accidentally at a great city entertainment, we found ourselves so mutually taken with one another, so acquainted, and so endeared between ourselves, that from thenceforward nothing was so near to us as one another. He wrote an excellent Latin satire, since printed, wherein he excuses the precipitation of our intelligence, so suddenly come to perfection, saying, that destined to have so short a continuance, as begun so late (for we were both full-grown men, and he some years the older), there was no time to lose, nor were we tied to conform to the example of those slow and regular friendships that require so many precautions of long preliminary conversation. This has no other idea than that of itself, and can only refer to itself: this is no one special consideration, nor two, nor three, nor four, nor a thousand; 'tis I know not what quintessence of all this mixture, which, seizing my whole will, carried it to plunge and lose itself in his, and that having seized his whole will, brought it back with equal concurrence and appetite to plunge and lose itself in mine. I may truly say lose, reserving nothing to ourselves, that was either his or mine.

When Laelius, in the presence of the Roman consuls, who after they had sentenced Tiberius Gracchus, prosecuted all those who had had any familiarity with him also, came to ask Caius Blosius, who was his chiefest friend, how much he would have done for him, and that he made answer: "All things." "How! All things!" said Laelius. "And what if he had commanded you to fire our temples?" "He would never have commanded me that," replied Blosius. "But what if he had?" said Laelius. "I would have obeyed him," said the other. If he was so perfect a friend to Gracchus, as the histories report him to have been, there was yet no necessity of offending the consuls by such a bold confession, though he might still have retained the assurance he had of Gracchus' disposition. However, those who accuse this answer as seditious, do not well understand the mystery; nor presuppose, as it was true, that he had Gracchus' will in his sleeve, both by the power of a friend, and the perfect knowledge he had of the man: they were more friends than citizens, more friends to one another than either friends or enemies to their country, or than friends to ambition and innovation; having absolutely given up themselves to one another, either held absolutely the reins of the other's inclination; and suppose all this guided by virtue, and all this by the conduct of reason, which also without these it had not been possible to do, Blosius' answer was such as it ought to be. If any of their actions flew out of the handle, they were neither (according to my measure of friendship) friends to one another, nor to themselves.

As to the rest, this answer carries no worse sound, than mine would do to one that should ask me: "If your will should command you to kill your daughter, would you do it?" and that I should make answer, that I would; for this expresses no consent to such an act, forasmuch as I do not in the least suspect my own will, and as little that of such a friend. 'Tis not in the power of all the eloquence in the world to dispossess me of the certainty I have of the intentions and resolutions of my friend: nay, no one action of his, what face soever it might bear, could be presented to me, of which I could not presently, and at first sight, find out the moving cause. Our souls had drawn so unanimously together, they had considered each other with so ardent an affection, and with the like affection laid open the very bottom of our hearts to one another's view, that I not only knew his as well as my own; but should certainly in any concern of mine have trusted my interest much more willingly with him than with myself.

Let no one, therefore, rank other common friendships with such a one as this. I have had as much experience of these as another, and of the most perfect of their kind; but I do not advise that any should confound the rules of the one and the other, for they would find themselves much deceived. In those other ordinary friendships, you are to walk with bridle in your hand, with prudence and circumspection, for in them the knot is not so sure, that a man may not half suspect it will slip. "Love him," said Chilo, "so, as if you were one day to hate him; and hate him so, as you were one day to love him." This precept, though abominable in the sovereign and perfect friendship I speak of, is nevertheless very sound, as to the practice of the ordinary and customary ones, and to which the saying that Aristotle had so frequent in his mouth, "Oh, my friends, there is no friend;" may very fitly be applied.

In this noble commerce, good offices, presents, and benefits, by which other friendships are supported and maintained, do not deserve so much as to be mentioned, and the reason is the concurrence of our wills; for as the kindness I have for myself receives no increase, for anything I relieve myself withal in time of need (whatever the Stoics say), and as I do not find myself obliged to myself for any service I do myself: so the union of such friends, being truly perfect, deprives them of all idea of such duties, and makes them loathe and banish from their conversation these words of division and distinction, benefit, obligation, acknowledgment, entreaty, thanks, and the like. All things, wills, thoughts, opinions, goods, wives, children, honors, and lives, being in effect common between them, and that absolute concurrence of affections being no other than one soul in two bodies (according to that very proper definition of Aristotle), they can neither lend nor give anything to one another. This is the reason why the lawgivers, to honor marriage with some resemblance of this divine alliance, interdict all gifts between man and wife; inferring by that, that all should belong to each of them, and that they have nothing to divide or to give to each other.

If, in the friendship of which I speak, one could give to the other, the receiver of the benefit would be the man that obliged his friend; for each of them contending and above all things studying how to be useful to the other, he that administers the occasion is the liberal man, in giving his friend the satisfaction of doing that toward him, which above all things he most desires. When the philosopher Diogenes wanted money, he used to say that he redemanded it of his friends, not that he demanded it. And to let you see the practical working of this, I will here produce an ancient and singular example: Eudamidas a Corinthian had two friends, Charixenus a Sycionian, and Areteus a Corinthian; this man coming to die, being poor, and his two friends rich, he made his will after this manner. "I bequeath to Areteus the maintenance of my mother, to support and provide for her in her old age; and to Charixenus I bequeath the care of marrying my daughter, and to give her as good a portion as he is able; and in case one of these chance to die, I hereby substitute the survivor in his place." They who first saw this will, made themselves very merry at the contents: but the legatees being made acquainted with it, accepted it with very great content; and one of them, Charixenus, dying within five days after, and Areteus, by that means, having the charge of both duties devolved solely to him, he nourished the old woman with very great care and tenderness, and of five talents he had in estate, he gave two and a half in marriage with an only daughter he had of his own, and two and a half in marriage with the daughter of Eudamidas, and in one and the same day solemnized both their nuptials.

This example is very full, if one thing were not to be objected, namely, the multitude of friends: for the perfect friendship I speak of is indivisible; each one gives himself so entirely to his friend, that he has nothing left to distribute to others: on the contrary, is sorry that he is not double, treble, or quadruple, and that he has not many souls, and many wills, to confer them all upon this one object. Common friendships will admit of division; one may love the beauty of this person, the good-humor of that, the liberality of a third, the paternal affection of a fourth, the fraternal love of a fifth, and so of the rest: but this friendship that possesses the whole soul, and there rules and sways with an absolute sovereignty, cannot possibly admit of a rival. If two at the same time should call to you for succor, to which of them would you run? Should they require of you contrary offices, how could you serve them both? Should one commit a thing to your silence, that it were of importance to the other to know, how would you disengage yourself?

A unique and particular friendship dissolves all other obligations whatsoever: the secret I have sworn not to reveal to any other, I may without perjury communicate to him who is not another, but myself.

'Tis miracle enough certainly, for a man to double himself, and those that talk of tripling, talk they know not of what. Nothing is extreme, that has its like; and he who shall suppose, that of two, I love one as much as the other, that they mutually love one another too, and love me as much as I love them, multiplies into a confraternity the most single of units, and whereof, moreover, one alone is the hardest thing in the world to find. The rest of this story suits very well with what I was saying; for Eudamidas, as a bounty and favor, bequeaths to his friends a legacy of employing themselves in his necessity; he leaves them heirs to this liberality of his, which consists in giving them the opportunity of conferring a benefit upon him; and doubtless, the force of friendship is more eminently apparent in this act of his, than in that of Areteus.

In short, these are effects not to be imagined nor comprehended by such as have not experience of them, and which make me infinitely honor and admire the answer of that young soldier to Cyrus, by whom being asked how much he would take for a horse with which he had won the prize of a race, and whether he would exchange him for a kingdom? "No, truly, sir," said he, "but I would give him with all my heart, to get thereby a true friend, could I find out any man worthy of that alliance." He did not say ill in saying, "could I find"; for though one may almost everywhere meet with men sufficiently qualified for a superficial acquaintance, yet in this, where a man is to deal from the very bottom of his heart, without any manner of reservation, it will be requisite that all the wards and springs be truly wrought, and perfectly sure.

In confederations that hold but by one end, we are only to provide against the imperfections that particularly concern that end. It can be of no importance to me of what religion my physician or my lawyer is; this consideration has nothing in common with the offices of friendship which they owe me; and I am of the same indifference in the domestic acquaintance my servants must necessarily contract with me. I never inquire, when I am to take a footman, if he be chaste, but if he be diligent; and am not solicitous if my muleteer be given to gaming, as if he be strong and able; or if my cook be a swearer, if he be a good cook. I do not take upon me to direct what other men should do in the government of their families (there are plenty that meddle enough with that), but only give an account of my method in my own. Terence says, "This has been my way; as for you, do as you think fit."

For table-talk, I prefer the pleasant and witty before the learned and the grave; in bed, beauty before goodness; in common discourse, the ablest speaker, whether or no there be sincerity in the case. And, as he that was found astride upon a hobby-horse, playing with his children, entreated the person who had surprised him in that posture to say nothing of it till himself came to be a father, supposing that the fondness that would then possess his own soul, would render him a fairer judge of such an action; so I, also, could wish to speak to such as have had experience of what I say: though, knowing how remote a thing such a friendship is from the common practice, and how rarely it is to be found, I despair of meeting with any such judge. For even these discourses left us by antiquity upon this subject, seem to me flat and poor in comparison of the sense I have of it, and in this particular, the effects surpass even the precepts of philosophy. "While I have sense left to me, there will never be anything more acceptable to me than an agreeable friend" [Horace].

The ancient Menander declared him to be happy that had had the good fortune to meet with but the shadow of a friend: and doubtless he had good reason to say so, especially if he spoke by experience; for in good earnest, if I compare all the rest of my life, though, thanks be to God, I have passed my time pleasantly enough, and at my ease, and the loss of such a friend excepted, free from any grievous affliction, and in great tranquillity of mind, having been contented with my natural and original commodities, without being solicitous after others; if I should compare it all, I say, with the four years I had the happiness to enjoy the sweet society of this excellent man, 'tis nothing but smoke, an obscure and tedious night. From the day that I lost him, "A day to me forever sad, forever sacred, so have you willed, ye gods" [*Aeneid*], I have only led a languishing life; and the very pleasures that present themselves to me, instead of administering anything of consolation, double my affliction for his loss. We were halves throughout, and to that degree, that methinks, by outliving him, I defraud him of his part. "I have determined that it will never be right for me to enjoy any pleasure, so long as he, with whom I shared in all pleasures, is away" [Terence].

I was so grown and accustomed to be always his double in all places and in all things, that methinks I am no more than half of myself. As Horace says: "If that half of my soul were snatched away from me by an untimely stroke, why should the other stay? That which remains will not be equally dear, will not be a whole: the same day will involve the destruction of both." There is no action or imagination of mine wherein I do not miss him; as I know that he would

157

have missed me: for as he surpassed me by infinite degrees in virtue and all other accomplishments, so he also did in the duties of friendship. "What shame can there be, or measure, in lamenting so dear a friend?"

LUCY MAUD MONTGOMERY
1874–1942

Since Anne Shirley's first appearance in 1908, Lucy
Maud Montgomery's spunky Canadian orphan has
made friends with generations of readers worldwide.
Prince Edward Island, where Montgomery and her
heroine spent their childhoods, is a pilgrimage site
for millions of visitors. As a child, Montgomery
escaped into her imagination by making up stories.
By her mid-twenties, she was earning her living as
an internationally published author, writing nearly
1,000 poems and short stories and ten volumes of
personal diaries over the course of her career. Montgomery's depiction of wilful optimism in the face of
adversity earned her legions of fans. Her international honours include an OBE. *Anne of Green
Gables* was the first of a series of satires of straight-
laced provincial life. With impish charm, Anne
confides her loneliness and her heartfelt wish for 'a
really kindred spirit' in the chapter excerpted here.

from *Anne of Green Gables*

CHAPTER VIII.

ANNE'S BRINGING-UP IS BEGUN

For reasons best known to herself, Marilla did not tell Anne that she was to stay at Green Gables until the next afternoon. During the forenoon she kept the child busy with various tasks and watched over her with a keen eye while she did them. By noon she had concluded that Anne was smart and obedient, willing to work and quick to learn; her most serious shortcoming seemed to be a tendency to fall into daydreams in the middle of a task and forget all about it until such time as she was sharply recalled to earth by a reprimand or a catastrophe.

When Anne had finished washing the dinner dishes she suddenly confronted Marilla with the air and expression of one desperately determined to learn the worst. Her thin little body trembled from head to foot; her face flushed and her eyes dilated until they were almost black; she clasped her hands tightly and said in an imploring voice:

"Oh, please, Miss Cuthbert, won't you tell me if you are going to send me away or not? I've tried to be patient all the morning, but I really feel that I cannot bear not knowing any longer. It's a dreadful feeling. Please tell me."

"You haven't scalded the dish-cloth in clean hot water as I told you to do," said Marilla immovably. "Just go and do it before you ask any more questions, Anne."

Anne went and attended to the dish-cloth. Then she returned to Marilla and fastened imploring eyes on the latter's face.

"Well," said Marilla, unable to find any excuse for deferring her explanation longer, "I suppose I might as well tell you. Matthew and I have decided to keep you—that is, if you will try to be a good little girl and show yourself grateful. Why, child, whatever is the matter?"

"I'm crying," said Anne in a tone of bewilderment. "I can't think why. I'm glad as glad can be. Oh, *glad* doesn't seem the right word at all. I was glad about the White Way and the cherry blossoms—but this! Oh, it's something more than glad. I'm so happy. I'll try to be so good. It will be up-hill work, I expect, for Mrs. Thomas often told me I was desperately wicked. However, I'll do my very best. But can you tell me why I'm crying?"

"I suppose it's because you're all excited and worked up," said Marilla disapprovingly. "Sit down on that chair and try to calm yourself. I'm afraid you both cry and laugh far too easily. Yes, you can stay here and we will try to do right by you. You must go to school; but it's only a fortnight till vacation so it isn't worth while for you to start before it opens again in September."

"What am I to call you?" asked Anne. "Shall I always say Miss Cuthbert? Can I call you Aunt Marilla?"

"No; you'll call me just plain Marilla. I'm not used to being called Miss Cuthbert and it would make me nervous."

"It sounds awfully disrespectful to say just Marilla," protested Anne.

"I guess there'll be nothing disrespectful in it if you're careful to speak respectfully. Everybody, young and old, in Avonlea calls me Marilla except the minister. He says Miss Cuthbert—when he thinks of it."

"I'd love to call you Aunt Marilla," said Anne wistfully. "I've never had an aunt or any relation at all—not even a grandmother. It would make me feel as if I really belonged to you. Can't I call you Aunt Marilla?"

"No. I'm not your aunt and I don't believe in calling people names that don't belong to them."

"But we could imagine you were my aunt."

"I couldn't," said Marilla grimly.

"Do you never imagine things different from what they really are?" asked Anne wide-eyed.

"No."

"Oh!" Anne drew a long breath. "Oh, Miss—Marilla, how much you miss!"

"I don't believe in imagining things different from what they really are," retorted Marilla. "When the Lord puts us in certain circumstances He doesn't mean for us to imagine them away. And that reminds me. Go into the sitting-room, Anne—be sure your feet are clean and don't let any flies in—and bring me out the illustrated card that's on the mantelpiece. The Lord's Prayer is on it and you'll devote your spare time this afternoon to learning it off by heart. There's to be no more of such praying as I heard last night."

"I suppose I was very awkward," said Anne apologetically, "but then, you see, I'd never had any practice. You couldn't really expect a person to pray very well the first time she tried, could you? I thought out a splendid prayer after I went to bed, just as I promised you I would. It was nearly as long as a minister's and so poetical. But would you believe it? I couldn't remember one word when I woke up this morning. And I'm afraid I'll never be able to think out another one as good. Somehow, things never are so good when they're thought out a second time. Have you ever noticed that?"

"Here is something for you to notice, Anne.

When I tell you to do a thing I want you to obey me at once and not stand stock-still and discourse about it. Just you go and do as I bid you."

Anne promptly departed for the sitting-room across the hall; she failed to return; after waiting ten minutes Marilla laid down her knitting and marched after her with a grim expression. She found Anne standing motionless before a picture hanging on the wall between the two windows, with her hands clasped behind her, her face uplifted, and her eyes astar with dreams. The white and green light strained through apple-trees and clustering vines outside fell over the rapt little figure with a half-unearthly radiance.

"Anne, whatever are you thinking of?" demanded Marilla sharply.

Anne came back to earth with a start.

"That," she said, pointing to the picture—a rather vivid chromo entitled, "Christ Blessing Little Children"—"and I was just imagining I was one of them—that I was the little girl in the blue dress, standing off by herself in the corner as if she didn't belong to anybody, like me. She looks lonely and sad, don't you think? I guess she hadn't any father or mother of her own. But she wanted to be blessed, too, so she just crept shyly up on the outside of the crowd, hoping nobody would notice her—except

Him. I'm sure I know just how she felt. Her heart must have beat and her hands must have got cold, like mine did when I asked you if I could stay. She was afraid He mightn't notice her. But it's likely He did, don't you think? I've been trying to imagine it all out—her edging a little nearer all the time until she was quite close to Him; and then He would look at her and put His hand on her hair and oh, such a thrill of joy as would run over her! But I wish the artist hadn't painted Him so sorrowful-looking. All His pictures are like that, if you've noticed. But I don't believe He could really have looked so sad or the children would have been afraid of Him."

"Anne," said Marilla, wondering why she had not broken into this speech long before, "you shouldn't talk that way. It's irreverent—positively irreverent."

Anne's eyes marvelled.

"Why, I felt just as reverent as could be. I'm sure I didn't mean to be irreverent."

"Well, I don't suppose you did—but it doesn't sound right to talk so familiarly about such things. And another thing, Anne, when I send you after something you're to bring it at once and not fall into mooning and imagining before pictures. Remember that. Take that card and come right to the kitchen. Now, sit down in the corner and learn that prayer off by heart."

Anne set the card up against the jugful of apple blossoms she had brought in to decorate the dinner-table—Marilla had eyed that decoration askance, but had said nothing—propped her chin on her hands, and fell to studying it intently for several silent minutes.

"I like this," she announced at length. "It's beautiful. I've heard it before—I heard the superintendent of the asylum Sunday-school say it over once. But I didn't like it then. He had such a cracked voice and he prayed it so mournfully. I really felt sure he thought praying was a disagreeable duty. This isn't poetry, but it makes me feel just the same way poetry does. 'Our Father who art in heaven, hallowed be Thy name.' That is just like a line of music. Oh, I'm so glad you thought of making me learn this, Miss—Marilla."

"Well, learn it and hold your tongue," said Marilla shortly.

Anne tipped the vase of apple blossoms near enough to bestow a soft kiss on a pink-cupped bud, and then studied diligently for some moments longer.

"Marilla," she demanded presently, "do you think that I shall ever have a bosom friend in Avonlea?"

"A—a what kind of a friend?"

"A bosom friend—an intimate friend, you know—a really kindred spirit to whom I can confide my inmost soul. I've dreamed of meeting her all my life. I never really supposed I would, but so many of my loveliest dreams have come true all at once that perhaps this one will, too. Do you think it's possible?"

"Diana Barry lives over at Orchard Slope and she's about your age. She's a very nice little girl, and perhaps she will be a playmate for you when she comes home. She's visiting her aunt over at Carmody just now. You'll have to be careful how you behave yourself, though. Mrs. Barry is a very particular woman. She won't let Diana play with any little girl who isn't nice and good."

Anne looked at Marilla through the apple blossoms, her eyes aglow with interest.

"What is Diana like? Her hair isn't red, is it? Oh, I hope not. It's bad enough to have red hair myself, but I positively couldn't endure it in a bosom friend."

"Diana is a very pretty little girl. She has black eyes and hair and rosy cheeks. And she is good and smart, which is better than being pretty."

Marilla was as fond of morals as the Duchess in Wonderland, and was firmly convinced that one should be tacked on to every remark made to a child who was being brought up.

But Anne waved the moral inconsequently aside and seized only on the delightful possibilities before it.

"Oh, I'm so glad she's pretty. Next to being beautiful oneself—and that's impossible in my case—it would be best to have a beautiful bosom friend. When I lived with Mrs. Thomas she had a bookcase in her sitting-room with glass doors. There weren't any books in it; Mrs. Thomas kept her best china and her preserves there—when she had any preserves to keep. One of the doors was broken. Mr. Thomas smashed it one night when he was slightly intoxicated. But the other was whole and I used to pretend that my reflection in it was another little girl who lived in it. I called her Katie Maurice, and we were very intimate. I used to talk to her by the hour, especially on Sunday, and tell her everything. Katie was the comfort and consolation of my life. We used to pretend that the bookcase was enchanted and that if I only knew the spell I could open the door and step right into the room where Katie Maurice lived, instead of into Mrs. Thomas' shelves of preserves and china. And then Katie Maurice would have taken me by the hand and led me out into a wonderful place, all flowers and sunshine and fairies, and we would have lived there happy for ever after. When I went to live with Mrs. Hammond it just broke my heart to leave Katie Maurice. She felt it dreadfully, too, I know she did, for she was crying when she kissed me good-bye through the bookcase door. There was no bookcase at Mrs. Hammond's. But just up the river a little way from the house there was a long green little valley, and the loveliest echo lived there. It echoed back every word you said, even if you didn't talk a bit loud. So I imagined that it was a little girl called Violetta and we were great friends and I loved her almost as well as I loved Katie Maurice—not quite, but almost, you know. The night before I went to the asylum I said good-bye to Violetta, and oh, her good-bye came back to me in such sad, sad tones. I had become so attached to her that I hadn't the heart to imagine a bosom friend at the asylum, even if there had been any scope for imagination there."

"I think it's just as well there wasn't," said Marilla drily. "I don't approve of such goings-on. You seem to half believe your own imaginations. It will be well for you to have a real live friend to put such non-sense out of your head. But don't let Mrs. Barry hear you talking about your Katie Maurices and your Violettas or she'll think you tell stories."

"Oh, I won't. I couldn't talk of them to

everybody—their memories are too sacred for that. But I thought I'd like to have you know about them. Oh, look, here's a big bee just tumbled out of an apple blossom. Just think what a lovely place to live—in an apple blossom! Fancy going to sleep in it when the wind was rocking it. If I wasn't a human girl I think I'd like to be a bee and live among the flowers."

"Yesterday you wanted to be a sea-gull," sniffed Marilla. "I think you are very fickle-minded. I told you to learn that prayer and not talk. But it seems impossible for you to stop talking if you've got anybody that will listen to you. So go up to your room and learn it."

"Oh, I know it pretty nearly all now—all but just the last line."

"Well, never mind, do as I tell you. Go to your room and finish learning it well, and stay there until I call you down to help me get tea."

"Can I take the apple blossoms with me for company?" pleaded Anne.

"No; you don't want your room cluttered up with flowers. You should have left them on the tree in the first place."

"I did feel a little that way, too," said Anne. "I kind of felt I shouldn't shorten their lovely lives by picking them—I wouldn't want to be picked if I were an apple blossom. But the temptation was *irresistible*. What do you do when you meet with an irresistible temptation?"

"Anne, did you hear me tell you to go to your room?"

Anne sighed, retreated to the east gable, and sat down in a chair by the window.

"There—I know this prayer. I learned that last sentence coming up-stairs. Now I'm going to imagine things into this room so that they'll always stay imagined. The floor is covered with a white velvet carpet with pink roses all over it and there are pink silk curtains at the windows. The walls are hung with gold and silver brocade tapestry. The furniture is mahogany. I never saw any mahogany, but it does sound *so* luxurious. This is a couch all heaped with gorgeous silken cushions, pink and blue and crimson and gold, and I am reclining gracefully on it. I can see my reflection in that splendid big mirror hanging on the wall. I am tall and regal, clad in a gown of trailing white lace, with a pearl cross on my breast and pearls in my hair. My hair is of midnight darkness and my skin is a clear ivory pallor. My name is the Lady Cordelia Fitzgerald. No, it isn't— I can't make *that* seem real."

She danced up to the little looking-glass and

peered into it. Her pointed freckled face and solemn gray eyes peered back at her.

"You're only Anne of Green Gables," she said earnestly, "and I see you, just as you are looking now, whenever I try to imagine I'm the Lady Cordelia. But it's a million times nicer to be Anne of Green Gables than Anne of nowhere in particular, isn't it?"

She bent forward, kissed her reflection affectionately, and betook herself to the open window.

"Dear Snow Queen, good afternoon. And good afternoon, dear birches down in the hollow. And good afternoon, dear gray house up on the hill. I wonder if Diana is to be my bosom friend. I hope she will, and I shall love her very much. But I must never quite forget Katie Maurice and Violetta. They would feel so hurt if I did and I'd hate to hurt anybody's feelings, even a little bookcase girl's or a little echo girl's. I must be careful to remember them and send them a kiss every day."

Anne blew a couple of airy kisses from her fingertips past the cherry blossoms and then, with her chin in her hands, drifted luxuriously out on a sea of day-dreams.

❦

ANNE ISABELLA
THACKERAY RITCHIE
1837–1919

Ritchie achieved success as a novelist and essayist in the second half of the nineteenth century. Much admired for *Mrs. Dymond*, *The Village on the Cliff* and *Old Kensington*, her fiction writing made use of autobiography as well as contemporary English and European history, occasionally resorting to popular literary styles including melodrama. She is less well known today than her novelist father, William Makepeace Thackeray, and her niece, Virginia Woolf, who eulogized Ritchie for having written 'passages which can only be matched in the classics.' Henry James credited Ritchie with having 'the power to guess the unseen from the seen' and George Eliot deemed her one of the few modern novelists worth reading. Her reminiscences of Tennyson, Ruskin, the Brownings and other literary friends chronicled a vanishing Victorian era. In the essay that follows, from *Toilers and Spinsters*, Ritchie uses her personal experience to reflect on friendship from the point of view of both an older and a younger woman.

'In Friendship'

Il faut dans ce bas monde aimer beaucoup de choses,
　　Pour savoir après tout ce qu'on aime le mieux . . .
Il faut fouler au pieds des fleurs à peine écloses;
　　Il faut beaucoup pleurer, dire beaucoup d'adieux . . .
De ces biens passagers que l'on goûte à demi
　　Le meilleur qui nous reste est un ancien ami—

So says Alfred de Musset, in his sonnet to Victor
Hugo: and as we live on we find out who are in truth
the people that we have really loved, which of our
companions belongs to us, linked in friendship as
well as by the chances of life or relationship. Sometimes it is not until they are gone that we discover
who and what they were to us—those 'good friends
and true' with whom we were at ease, tranquil in the
security of their kind presence.

Some of us, the longer we live, only feel more and
more that it is not in utter loneliness that the greatest peace is to be found. A little child starts up in the
dark, and finding itself alone, begins to cry and toss
in its bed, as it holds out its arms in search of a
protecting hand; and men and women seem for the
most part true to this first childish instinct as they
awaken suddenly: (how strange these awakenings
are, in what incongruous places and seasons do they

come to us!) People turn helplessly, looking here and there for protection, for sympathy, for affection, for charity of human fellowship; give it what name you like, it is the same cry for companionship, and terror of the death of silence and absence. Human Sympathy, represented by inadequate words, or by clumsy exaggeration, by feeble signs or pangs innumerable, by sudden glories and unreasonable ecstasies, is, when we come to think of it, among the most reasonable of emotions. It is life indeed; it binds us to the spirit of our race as our senses bind us to the material world, and makes us feel at times as if we were indeed a part of Nature herself, and chords responding to her touch.

People say that as a rule men are truer friends than women—more capable of friendship. Is this the result of a classical education? Do the foot-notes in which celebrated friendships are mentioned in brackets stimulate our youth to imitate those stately togas, whose names and discourses come travelling down to us through two thousand years, from one country to another, from one generation to another, from one language to another, until they flash perhaps into the pages of Bohn's Classical Library, of which a volume has been lent to me from the study-table on the hill? It is lying open at the chapter on friendship. 'To me, indeed, though he was snatched away, Scipio still lives, and will always live; for I love the virtue of a man, and assuredly of all things that either fortune or nature has bestowed upon me, I have none which I can compare with the friendship of Scipio.' So says Cicero, speaking by the mouth of Laelius and of Bohn, and the generous thought still lives after many a transmigration, though it exists now in a world where perhaps friendship is less thought of than in the days when Scipio was mourned. Some people have a special gift of their own for friendship; they transform a vague and abstract feeling for us into an actual voice and touch and response. As our life flows on—'a torrent of impressions and emotions bounded in by custom,' a writer calls it whose own deep torrent has long since overflowed any narrow confining boundaries—the mere names of our friends might for many of us almost tell the history of our own lives. As one thinks over the roll, each name seems a fresh sense and explanation to the past. Some, which seem to have outwardly but little influence on our fate, tell for us the whole hidden story of long years. One means perhaps passionate emotion, unreasonable reproach, tender reconciliation; another may mean injustice, forgiveness, remorse; while another speaks to us of all that we have ever suffered, all that we hold most sacred in life, and gratitude and trust unfailing.

There is one name that seems to me like the music of Bach as I think of it, and another that seems to open at the Gospel of St. Matthew. 'My dearest friend,' a young man wrote to his mother only yesterday, and the simple words seemed to me to tell the whole history of their lives.

'After these two noble fruits of friendship, peace in the affections, and support of the judgment, followeth the last fruit, which is like the pomegranate, full of many kernels. I mean aid and bearing a part in all actions and occasions,' says Lord Bacon, writing in the spirit of Cicero three hundred years ago.

To be in love is a recognised state; relationship without friendship is perhaps too much recognised in civilised communities; but friendship, that best blessing of life, seems to have less space in its scheme than almost any other feeling of equal importance. Of course it has its own influence; but the outward life appears, on the whole, more given to business, to acquaintance, to ambition, to eating and drinking, than to the friends we really love: and time passes, and convenience takes us here and there, and work and worry (that we might have shared) absorb us, and one day time is no more for our friendship.

One or two of my readers will understand why it is that I have been thinking of friendship of late, and have chosen this theme for my little essay, thinking that not the least lesson in life is surely that of human sympathy, and that to be a good friend is one of the secrets that comprise most others. And yet the sacrifices that we usually make for a friend's comfort or assistance are ludicrous when one comes to think of them. 'One mina, two minae; are there settled values for friends, Antisthenes, as there are for slaves? For of slaves one is perhaps worth two minae, another not even half a mina, another five minae, another ten.' Antisthenes agrees, and says that some friends are not even worth half a mina; 'and another,' he says, 'I would buy for my friend at the sacrifice of all the money and revenues in the world.'

I am afraid that we modern Antisthenes would think a month's income a serious sacrifice. If a friend is in trouble, we leave a card at his door, or go the length of a note, perhaps. And when all is well, we go our way silent and preoccupied. We absent ourselves for months at a time without a reason, and yet all of this is more want of habit than of feeling; for, notwithstanding all that is said of the world and its pompous vanities, there are still human beings among us, and, even after two thousand years, true things seem to come to life again and again for each one of us, in this sorrow and that happiness, in one sympathy and another; and one day a vague essay upon friendship becomes the true story of a friend.

In this peaceful island from whence I write we hear Cicero's voice, or listen to *In Memoriam*, as the Friend sings to us of friendship to the tune of the lark's shrill voice, or of the wave that beats away our holiday and dashes itself upon the rocks in the little bay. The sweet scents and dazzles of sunshine seem to harmonise with emotions that are wise and natural, and it is not until we go back to our common life that we realise the difference between the teaching of noble souls and the noisy bewildered translation into life of that solemn printed silence.

> Is it, then, regret for buried time,
> That keenlier in sweet April wakes,
> And meets the year, and gives and takes
> The colours of the crescent prime?
> Not all: the songs, the stirring air,
> The life re-orient out of dust,
> Cry thro' the scene to hearten trust
> In that which made the world so fair.

Here, then, and at peace, and out of doors in the spring-time, we have leisure to ask ourselves whether there is indeed some failure in the scheme of friendship and in the plan of that busy to-day in which our lives are passed; over-crowded with people, with repetition, with passing care and worry, and unsorted material. It is perhaps possible that by feeling and feeling alone, some check may be given to the trivial rush of meaningless repetition by which our time is frittered away, our precious power of love and passionate affection given to the winds.

Sometimes we suddenly realise for the first time the sense of kindness, the treasure of faithful protection that we have unconsciously owed for years, for our creditor has never claimed payment or reward, and we remember with natural emotion and gratitude that the time for payment is past; we shall be debtors all our lives long—debtors made richer by one man's generosity and liberal friendship, as we may be any day made poorer in heart by unkindness or want of truth.

Only a few weeks ago a friend passed from among us whose name for many, for the writer among the rest, spoke of a whole chapter in life, one of those good chapters to which we go back again and again. This friend was one of those who make a home of life for others, a home to which we all felt that we might come sure of a wise and unfailing welcome. The door opens, the friend comes in slowly with a welcoming smile on his pale and noble face. Where find more delightful companionship than

his? We all know the grace of that charming impro-
vised gift by which he seemed able to combine dis-
jointed hints and shades into a whole, to weave our
crude talk and ragged suggestions into a complete
scheme of humorous or more serious philosophy. In
some papers published a few years ago in the 'Corn-
hill Magazine,' called 'Chapters on Talk,' a great deal
of his delightful and pleasant humour appears.

But it was even more in his society than in his
writing that our friend showed himself as he was.
His talking was unlike that of anybody else; it sometimes put me in mind of another voice out of the
past. There was an earnest wit, a gentle audacity and
simplicity of expression, that made it come home to
us all. Of late, E. R. was saying he spoke with a quiet
and impressive authority that we all unconsciously
acknowledged, although we did not know that the
end of pain was near.

Of his long sufferings he never complained. But
if he spoke of himself, it was with some kind little
joke or humorous conceit and allusion to the philosophy of endurance, nor was it until after his death
that we knew what his martyrdom had been, nor
with what courage he had borne it.

He thought of serious things very constantly,
although not in the conventional manner. One of the
last times that we met he said to me, 'I feel more and

more convinced that the love of the Father is not unlike that of an earthly father; and that as an earthly father, so He rejoices in the prosperity and material well-doing of his children.' Another time, quoting from the 'Roundabout Papers,' he said suddenly, '"Be good, my dear." Depend upon it, that is the whole philosophy of life; it is very simple.'

Speaking of a friend, he said with some emotion, 'I think I love M. as well as if he were dead.'

He had a fancy, that we all used to laugh over with him, of a great central building, something like the Albert Hall, for friends to live in together, with galleries for the sleepless to walk in at night.

Perhaps some people may think that allusions so personal as these are scarcely fitted for these pages; but what is there in truth more unpersonal than the thought of a wise and gentle spirit, of a generous and truthful life? Here is a life that belongs to us all; we have all been the better for the existence of the one man. He could not be good without doing good in his generation, nor speak the truth as he did without adding to the sum of true things. And the lesson that he taught us was—'Let us be true to ourselves; do not let us be afraid to be ourselves, to love each other and to speak and to trust in each other.'

Last night the moon rose very pale at first, then blushing flame-like through the drifting vapours as they rose far beyond the downs; a great blackbird sat watching the shifting shadowy worlds from the bare branch of a tree, and the colts in the field set off scampering. Later, about eleven o'clock, the mists had dissolved into a silent silver and nightingale-broken dream—in which were vaporous downs, moonlight, sweet sudden stars, and clouds drifting, like some slow flight of silver birds. L— took us to a little terrace at the end of his father's garden. All the kingdoms of the night lay spread before us, bounded by dreams. For a minute we stood listening to the sound of the monotonous wave, and then it ceased—and in the utter silence a cuckoo called, and then the nightingale began, and then the wave answered once more.

It will all be a dream to-morrow, as we stumble into the noise, and light, and work of life again. Monday comes commonplace, garish, and one can scarce believe in the mystical Sunday night. And yet this tranquil Sunday night is more true than the flashiest gas-lamp in Piccadilly. Natural things seem inspired at times, and beyond themselves, and to carry us upwards and beyond our gas-lamps; so do people seem revealed to us at times, and in the night, when all is peace.

OSCAR WILDE
1854–1900

Known for his Irish wit and decadent proclivities,
Wilde was a one-man centre of gravity around
which much of artistic Victorian society orbited.
Although his novel *The Picture of Dorian Gray* horri-
fied some, his tart essays and droll comedies
delighted many more, taking 1890s London by
storm and quickly conquering the world. At the
height of his success, his private affairs were put on
trial and he was sentenced to hard labour for gross
indecency. It was the scandal of the century and
defined his place as a gay icon. Overnight, he and
his family were ruined (he had two young sons with
his journalist wife, Constance). Friends instantly
discarded him. In his last days, he haunted Paris
cafes alone, a shadow of the popular dandy he had
been. 'The Devoted Friend', the grimly comic morality tale included here, explodes age-old pieties by
exposing pretend friends and their poor moral character. With friends like these, the story asks, who
needs enemies?

'The Devoted Friend'

One morning the old water-rat put his head out of his hole. He had bright beady eyes and stiff grey whiskers, and his tail was like a long bit of black indiarubber. The little ducks were swimming about in the pond, looking just like a lot of yellow canaries, and their mother, who was pure white with real red legs, was trying to teach them how to stand on their heads in the water.

'You will never be in the best society unless you can stand on your heads,' she kept saying to them; and every now and then she showed them how it was done. But the little ducks paid no attention to her. They were so young that they did not know what an advantage it is to be in society at all.

'What disobedient children!' cried the old water-rat, 'they really deserve to be drowned.'

'Nothing of the kind,' answered the duck, 'everyone must make a beginning, and parents cannot be too patient.'

'Ah! I know nothing about the feelings of parents,' said the water-rat. 'I am not a family man. In fact, I have never been married, and I never intend to be. Love is all very well in its way, but friendship is much higher. Indeed, I know of nothing in the world that is either nobler or rarer than a devoted friendship.'

'And what, pray, is your idea of the duties of a devoted friend?' asked a green linnet, who was sitting on a willow tree hard by, and had overheard the conversation.

'Yes, that is just what I want to know,' said the duck; and she swam away to the end of the pond, and stood upon her head, in order to give her children a good example.

'What a silly question!' cried the water-rat. 'I should expect my devoted friend to be devoted to me, of course.'

'And what would you do in return?' said the little bird, swinging upon a silver spray, and flapping his tiny wings.

'I don't understand you,' answered the water-rat.

'Let me tell you a story on the subject,' said the linnet.

'Is the story about me?' asked the water-rat. 'If so, I will listen to it, for I am extremely fond of fiction.'

'It is applicable to you,' answered the linnet and he flew down, and alighting upon the bank, he told the story of The Devoted Friend.

'Once upon a time,' said the linnet, 'there was an honest little fellow named Hans.'

'Was he very distinguished?' asked the water-rat.

'No,' answered the linnet, 'I don't think he was distinguished at all, except for his kind heart, and his funny, round, good-humoured face. He lived in a tiny cottage all by himself, and every day he worked in his garden. In all the countryside there was no garden so lovely as his. Sweet-williams grew there, and gilly-flowers, and shepherds'-purses, and fair-maids of France. There were damask roses and yellow roses, lilac crocuses and gold, purple violets and white. Columbine and ladysmock, marjoram and wild basil, the cowslip and the flower-de-luce, the daffodil and the clove-pink bloomed or blossomed in their proper order as the months went by, one flower taking another flower's place, so that there were always beautiful things to look at and pleasant odours to smell.

'Little Hans had a great many friends, but the most devoted friend of all was big Hugh the miller. Indeed, so devoted was the rich miller to little Hans, that he would never go by his garden without leaning over the wall and plucking a large nosegay, or a handful of sweet herbs, or filling his pockets with plums and cherries if it was the fruit season.

'"Real friends should have everything in common," the miller used to say, and little Hans nodded and smiled, and felt very proud of having a friend with such noble ideas.

'Sometimes, indeed, the neighbours thought it strange that the rich miller never gave little Hans anything in return, though he had a hundred sacks of flour stored away in his mill, and six milch cows, and a large flock of woolly sheep; but Hans never troubled his head about these things, and nothing gave him greater pleasure than to listen to all the wonderful things the miller used to say about the unselfishness of true friendship.

'So little Hans worked away in his garden. During the spring, the summer and the autumn he was very happy, but when the winter came, and he had no fruit or flowers to bring to the market, he suffered a good deal from cold and hunger, and often had to go to bed without any supper but a few dried pears or some hard nuts. In the winter, also, he was extremely lonely, as the miller never came to see him then.

'"There is no good in my going to see little Hans as long as the snow lasts," the miller used to say to his wife, "for when people are in trouble they should be left alone and not be bothered by visitors. That at least is my idea about friendship, and I am sure I am right. So I shall wait till the spring comes, and then I shall pay him a visit, and he will be able to give me a large basket of primroses, and that will make him so happy."

'"You are certainly very thoughtful about others," answered the Wife, as she sat in her comfortable armchair by the big pinewood fire; "very thoughtful indeed. It is quite a treat to hear you talk about friendship. I am sure the clergyman himself could not say such beautiful things as you do, though he does live in a three-storeyed house, and wear a gold ring on his little finger."

'"But could we not ask little Hans up here?" said the miller's youngest son. "If poor Hans is in trouble I will give him half my porridge, and show him my white rabbits."

'"What a silly boy you are!" cried the miller; "I really don't know what is the use of sending you to school. You seem not to learn anything. Why if little Hans came up here, and saw our warm fire, and our good supper, and our great cask of red wine, he might get envious, and envy is a most terrible thing, and would spoil anybody's nature. I certainly will not allow Hans' nature to be spoiled. I am his best friend, and I will always watch over him, and see that he is not led into any temptations. Besides, if Hans came here, he might ask me to let him have some flour on credit, and that I could not do. Flour is one thing, and friendship is another and they should not be confused. Why, the words are spelt differently, and mean quite different things. Everybody can see that."

' "How well you talk!" said the miller's wife pouring herself out a large glass of warm ale; "really I feel quite drowsy. It is just like being in church."

' "Lots of people act well," answered the miller, "but very few people talk well, which shows that talking is much the more difficult thing of the two and much the finer thing also;" and he looked sternly across the table at his little son, who felt so ashamed of himself that he hung his head down, and grew quite scarlet and began to cry into his tea. However, he was so young that you must excuse him.'

'Is that the end of the story?' asked the water-rat.

'Certainly not,' answered the linnet, 'that is the beginning.'

'Then you are quite behind the age,' said the water-rat. 'Every good storyteller nowadays starts with the end, and then goes on to the beginning, and concludes with the middle. That is the new method. I heard all about it the other day from a critic who was walking round the pond with a young man. He spoke of the matter at great length, and I am sure he must have been right, for he had blue spectacles and a bald head and whenever the young man made any remark, he always answered "Pooh!" But pray go on with your story. I like the miller immensely. I have all kinds of beautiful sentiments myself, so there is a great sympathy between us.'

'Well,' said the linnet, hopping now on one leg and now on the other, 'as soon as the winter was over, and the primroses began to open their pale yellow stars, the miller said to his wife that he would go down and see little Hans.

'"Why, what a good heart you have!" cried his wife; "you are always thinking of others. And mind you take the big basket with you for the flowers.'

'So the miller tied the sails of the windmill together with a strong iron chain, and went down the hill with the basket on his arm.

'"Good-morning, little Hans," said the miller.

'"Good-morning," said Hans, leaning on his spade, and smiling from ear to ear.

'"And how have you been all the winter?" said the miller.

'"Well, really," cried Hans, "it is very good of you to ask, very good indeed. I am afraid I had rather a hard time of it, but now the spring has come, and I am quite happy, and all my flowers are doing well."

'"We often talked of you during the winter, Hans," said the miller, "and wondered how you were getting on.'

'"That was kind of you," said Hans; "I was half afraid you had forgotten me."

'"Hans, I am surprised at you," said the miller; "friendship never forgets. That is the wonderful thing about it, but I am afraid you don't understand the poetry of life. How lovely your primroses are looking, by the by!"

'"They are certainly very lovely," said Hans, "and it is a most lucky thing for me that I have so many. I am going to bring them into the market and sell them to the burgomaster's daughter, and buy back my wheelbarrow with the money."

'"Buy back your wheelbarrow? You don't mean to say you have sold it? What a very stupid thing to do!"

'"Well, the fact is," said Hans, "that I was obliged to. You see the winter was a very bad time for me and I really had no money at all to buy bread with. So I first sold the silver buttons off my Sunday coat, and then I sold my silver chain, and then I sold my big pipe, and at last I sold my wheelbarrow. But I am going to buy them all back again now."

'"Hans," said the miller, "I will give you my wheelbarrow. It is not in very good repair; indeed, one side is gone, and there is something wrong with the wheel-spokes; but in spite of that I will give it to you. I know it is very generous of me, and a great many people would think me extremely foolish for parting with it, but I am not like the rest of the world. I think that generosity is the essence of friendship and, besides, I have got a new wheelbarrow for myself. Yes, you may set your mind at ease. I will give you my wheelbarrow."

'"Well, really, that is generous of you," said little Hans, and his funny round face glowed all over with pleasure. "I can easily put it in repair, as I have a plank of wood in the house."

'"A plank of wood!" said the miller, "why, that is just what I want for the roof of my barn. There is a very large hole in it, and the corn will all get damp if I don't stop it up. How lucky you mentioned it! It is quite remarkable how one good action always breeds another. I have given you my wheelbarrow, and now you are going to give me your plank. Of course, the wheelbarrow is worth far more than the plank, but true friendship never notices things like that. Pray get it at once, and I will set to work at my barn this very day."

'"Certainly," cried little Hans, and he ran into the shed and dragged the plank out.

'"It is not a very big plank," said the miller, looking at it, "and I am afraid that after I have mended my barn-roof there won't be any left for you to mend the wheelbarrow with; but, of course, that is not my fault. And now, as I have given you my wheelbarrow, I am sure you would like to give me some flowers in return. Here is the basket, and mind you fill it quite full."

'"Quite full?" said little Hans, rather sorrowfully, for it was really a very big basket, and he knew that if he filled it he would have no flowers left for the market, and he was very anxious to get his silver buttons back.

'"Well, really," answered the miller, "as I have given you my wheelbarrow, I don't think that it is much to ask you for a few flowers. I may be wrong but I should have thought that friendship, true friendship, was quite free from selfishness of any kind."

'"My dear friend, my best friend," cried little Hans, "you are welcome to all the flowers in my garden. I would much sooner have your good opinion than my silver buttons, any day," and he ran and plucked all his pretty primroses, and filled the miller's basket.

'"Goodbye, little Hans," said the miller, and he went up the hill with the plank on his shoulder, and the big basket in his hand.

'"Goodbye," said little Hans, and he began to dig away quite merrily, he was so pleased about the wheelbarrow.

'The next day he was nailing up some honeysuckle against the porch, when he heard the miller's voice calling to him from the road. So he jumped off the ladder, and ran down the garden, and looked over the wall.

'There was the miller with a large sack of flour on his back.

'"Dear little Hans," said the miller, "would you mind carrying this sack of flour for me to market?"

'"Oh, I am so sorry," said Hans, "but I am really very busy today. I have got all my creepers to nail up, and all my flowers to water and all my grass to roll."

'"Well, really," said the miller, "I think, that considering that I am going to give you my wheelbarrow it is rather unfriendly of you to refuse."

'"Oh don't say that," cried little Hans, "I wouldn't be unfriendly for the whole world;" and he ran in for his cap, and trudged off with the big sack on his shoulders.

'It was a very hot day and the road was terribly dusty and before Hans had reached the sixth milestone he was so tired that he had to sit down and rest. However, he went on bravely, and at last he reached the market. After he had waited there for some time, he sold the sack of flour for a very good price, and then he returned home at once, for he was afraid that if he stopped too late he might meet some robbers on the way.

'"It has certainly been a hard day," said little Hans to himself as he was going to bed, "but I am glad I did not refuse the miller, for he is my best friend and, besides, he is going to give me his wheel-barrow."

'Early the next morning the miller came down to get the money for his sack of flour, but little Hans was so tired that he was still in bed.

'"Upon my word," said the miller, "you are very lazy. Really, considering that I am going to give you my wheelbarrow, I think you might work harder. Idleness is a great sin, and I certainly don't like any of my friends to be idle or sluggish. You must not mind my speaking quite plainly to you. Of course, I should not dream of doing so if I were not your friend. But what is the good of friendship if one cannot say exactly what one means? Anybody can say charming things and try to please and to flatter, but a true friend always says unpleasant things, and does not mind giving pain. Indeed, if he is a really true friend he prefers it, for he knows that then he is doing good."

'"I am very sorry," said little Hans, rubbing his eyes and pulling off his nightcap, "but I was so tired that I thought I would lie in bed for a little time, and listen to the birds singing. Do you know that I always work better after hearing the birds sing?"

'"Well, I am glad of that," said the miller, clap-ping little Hans on the back, "for I want you to come up to the mill as soon as you are dressed and mend my barn-roof for me."

'Poor little Hans was very anxious to go and work in his garden, for his flowers had not been watered for two days, but he did not like to refuse the miller, as he was such a good friend to him.

'"Do you think it would be unfriendly of me if I said I was busy?" he enquired in a shy and timid voice.

'"Well, really,' answered the miller, "I do not think it is much to ask of you, considering that I am going to give you my wheelbarrow; but, of course, if you refuse I will go and do it myself. '

'"Oh! on no account," cried little Hans; and he jumped out of bed, and dressed himself, and went up to the barn.

'He worked there all day long, till sunset, and at sunset the miller came to see how he was getting on.

'"Have you mended the hole in the roof yet, little Hans?" cried the miller in a cheery voice.

'"It is quite mended," answered little Hans, coming down the ladder.

'"Ah!" said the miller, "there is no work so delightful as the work one does for others."

'"It is certainly a great privilege to hear you talk," answered little Hans, sitting down and wiping his forehead, "a very great privilege. But I am afraid I shall never have such beautiful ideas as you have."

'"Oh! they will come to you," said the miller, "but you must take more pains. At present you have only the practice of friendship; some day you will have the theory also."

'"Do you really think I shall?" asked little Hans.

'"I have no doubt of it," answered the miller, "but now that you have mended the roof, you had better go home and rest, for I want you to drive my sheep to the mountain tomorrow."

'Poor little Hans was afraid to say anything to this, and early the next morning the miller brought his sheep round to the cottage, and Hans started off with them to the mountain. It took him the whole day to get there and back; and when he returned he was so tired that he went off to sleep in his chair, and did not wake up till it was broad daylight.

'"What a delightful time I shall have in my garden!" he said, and he went to work at once.

'But somehow he was never able to look after his flowers at all, for his friend the miller was always coming round and sending him off on long errands or getting him to help at the mill. Little Hans was very much distressed at times as he was afraid his flowers would think he had forgotten them, but he consoled himself by the reflection that the miller was his best friend. "Besides," he used to say, "he is going to give me his wheelbarrow, and that is an act of pure generosity."

'So little Hans worked away for the miller, and the miller said all kinds of beautiful things about friendship, which Hans took down in a notebook, and used to read over at night, for he was a very good scholar.

'Now it happened that one evening little Hans was sitting by his fireside when a loud rap came at the door. It was a very wild night, and the wind was blowing and roaring round the house so terribly that at first he thought it was merely the storm. But a second rap came, and then a third, louder than any of the others.

'"It is some poor traveller," said little Hans to himself and he ran to the door.

'There stood the miller with a lantern in one hand and a big stick in the other.

'"Dear little Hans," cried the miller, "I am in great trouble. My little boy has fallen off a ladder and hurt himself, and I am going for the doctor. But he lives so far away, and it is such a bad night, that it has just occurred to me that it would be much better if you went instead of me. You know I am going to give you my wheelbarrow, and so it is only fair that you should do something for me in return."

'"Certainly," cried little Hans, "I take it quite as a compliment your coming to me, and I will start off at once. But you must lend me your lantern, as the night is so dark that I am afraid I might fall into the ditch."

'"I am very sorry," answered the miller, "but it is my new lantern, and it would be a great loss to me if anything happened to it."

'"Well, never mind, I will do without it," cried little Hans, and he took down his great fur coat, and his warm scarlet cap, and tied a muffler round his throat, and started off.

'What a dreadful storm it was! The night was so black that little Hans could hardly see, and the wind was so strong that he could hardly stand. However, he was very courageous, and after he had been walking about three hours, he arrived at the doctor's house, and knocked at the door.

'"Who is there?" cried the doctor, putting his head out of his bedroom window.

'"Little Hans, doctor."

'"What do you want, little Hans?"

'"The miller's son has fallen from a ladder, and has hurt himself, and the miller wants you to come at once."

'"All right!" said the doctor; and he ordered his horse, and his big boots, and his lantern, and came downstairs, and rode off in the direction of the miller's house, little Hans trudging behind him.

'But the storm grew worse and worse, and the rain fell in torrents, and little Hans could not see where he was going, or keep up with the horse. At last he lost his way, and wandered off on the moor, which was a very dangerous place, as it was full of deep holes, and there poor little Hans was drowned. His body was found the next day by some goatherds, floating in a great pool of water, and was brought back by them to the cottage.

'Everybody went to little Hans' funeral, as he was so popular, and the miller was the chief mourner.

'"As I was his best friend," said the miller, "it is only fair that I should have the best place," so he walked at the head of the procession in a long black cloak, and every now and then he wiped his eyes with a big pocket-handkerchief.

'"Little Hans is certainly a great loss to everyone," said the blacksmith, when the funeral was over, and they were all seated comfortably in the inn, drinking spiced wine and eating sweet cakes.

'"A great loss to me at any rate," answered the miller; "why, I had as good as given him my wheelbarrow, and now I really don't know what to do with it. It is very much in my way at home, and it is in such bad repair that I could not get anything for it if I sold it. I will certainly take care not to give away anything again. One certainly suffers for being generous."'

'Well?' said the water-rat, after a long pause.

'Well, that is the end,' said the linnet.

'But what became of the miller?' asked the water-rat.

'Oh! I really don't know,' replied the linnet; 'and I am sure that I don't care.'

'It is quite evident then that you have no sympathy in your nature,' said the water-rat.

'I am afraid you don't quite see the moral of the story,' remarked the linnet.

'The what?' screamed the water-rat.

'The moral.'

'Do you mean to say that the story has a moral?'

'Certainly,' said the linnet.

'Well, really,' said the water-rat, in a very angry manner, 'I think you should have told me that before you began. If you had done so, I certainly would not have listened to you; in fact, I should have said "Pooh", like the critic. However, I can say it now;' so he shouted out 'Pooh' at the top of his voice, gave a whisk with his tail, and went back into his hole.

'And how do you like the water-rat?' asked the duck, who came paddling up some minutes afterwards. 'He has a great many good points, but for my own part I have a mother's feelings and I can never look at a confirmed bachelor without the tears coming into my eyes.'

'I am rather afraid that I have annoyed him,' answered the linnet. 'The fact is that I told him a story with a moral.'

'Ah! that is always a very dangerous thing to do,' said the duck.

And I quite agree with her.